PLAIN JANE

PLAIN JANE

JOAN BARFOOT

MACMILLAN CANADA
TORONTO, ONTARIO, CANADA

Macmillan Canada wishes to thank the Canada Council for supporting its publishing program.

Canadian Cataloguing in Publication Data

Barfoot, Joan, 1946-
  Plain Jane

ISBN 0-7715-9157-8

I. Title

PS8553.A74P5 1992   C813′ .54   C92-093328-9
PR9199.3.B37P5 1992

Macmillan Canada
A Division of Canada Publishing Corporation
Toronto, Ontario, Canada

1 2 3 4 5   FP 96 95 94 93 92

Printed in Canada

PLAIN JANE

1

Jane Smith, not ordinarily a person of large event, is busy writing the letter that will change her life. Sitting on the edge of her loveseat in her living room, bent over her glass-topped coffee table, she finds herself searching for winning words. Jane's no writer of letters, or of much else, so this is quite a struggle.

It would come as no surprise to her to hear that this letter will change her life. More or less, that's why she's writing it, although she hasn't thought about what she's doing very carefully or, really, at all.

"July 23," she has written at the top of the page. And then, "Dear prisoner."

Dear prisoner!

Just moments ago, on what was still an ordinary evening, here was Jane on her loveseat in her living room, home from work and drinking tea and thumbing through the newspaper, reading idly. And her eye was caught, captured, there was a kind of turning over of her heart, and she stood right up to fetch paper from her bedside table, and sat right down again to write.

Jane doesn't normally care for surprises, but she has certainly embraced this one.

"Hi," she writes.

"My name is Jane Smith, and I saw your advertisement in the newspaper, so thought I would write. I'm sending this to your number because that's all your advertisement said, but it's hard to write to a number, even if a name doesn't actually tell you much, so if you answer, could you tell me your name?"

She is not herself. This is someone unfamiliar, brave and beyond herself. She feels daring, but also that she is in the grip of inevitability: that something romantic, exciting, even thrilling (in the way of the books she reads, nothing harsher) must come of this.

Well, these things do happen, don't they, these bolts from the psychic blue?

"My name really is Jane Smith, even though it sounds made up. My mother used to say that somebody has to be called that or it wouldn't be such an ordinary name. She used to say the thing to do with a name like that is to make yourself stand out anyway, but I don't know."

What she means is, her mother seems to have gone out of her way to make matters difficult for Jane; not to mention that her advice has seldom come close to touching Jane's experience. But that's hardly the sort of thing she would confide to someone who is, after all, a stranger. Nor is it the sort of complaining tone she wants to set.

"Anyway. I've never done anything like this before, and it's hard to write to somebody when you don't know him, not even his name, never mind anything else. Actually, if we met you might think I was quite a shy person, but I guess letters are different. There's only one side to them so you just have to keep talking and talking all on your own."

Oh dear, she is babbling. Still, she has so little to go on. Who knows what will appeal? What she feels is that she is seeing with new eyes and writing with fresh words.

"What would you like to know about me? I can tell you I'm single and work in a library, except I'm not exactly a librarian. I type things for people and send out notices when books and records are overdue, and do other administration kinds of jobs, and sometimes I put books back on the shelves, although there are other people who are supposed to do that."

How dull, Jane, and unimpressive! You'll have to make yourself sound more entrancing than that.

"I guess it doesn't sound very exciting, but it's okay and I have a nice apartment pretty well fixed up the way I like it, and I enjoy things like movies. Also I have several hobbies, such as reading (I like big fat books best) and knitting. Possibly if you sent me your measurements (like chest and neck size and arm length) I could make you a sweater sometime? That's if you want to answer this letter. I don't know what it must be like where you are. Are you very busy most of the time or not busy at all?"

This is hardly the most critical question she might be asking, is it?

"Anyway, I hope you'll write me back. Maybe you're getting lots of letters? If so, don't feel bad if you don't get time to respond to this." Although of course he will. He has to. Otherwise how could she have been so struck by inevitability?

"As I said, I saw your advertisement and thought I'd write. It caught my eye, I don't really know why. Do you ever get a feeling there's things you just have to do?"

It's possible he's quite familiar with that feeling. It's possible that's precisely what's landed him where he is, a matter of irresistible impulse, overwhelming desire.

"I bet when you put in an advertisement like that you get some weird answers! I just want you to know this isn't one of them, there was just something about your ad that

3

made me feel like writing, and I hope you'll feel like answering.

"Yours truly,

"Jane Smith."

In the end, these words aren't very satisfying, even to Jane. Who knows how he will interpret them? He may find their very dullness weird. Because to be where he is at all, his life must be a good deal more active than that of someone who works in a library and likes to knit and read.

Perhaps he will find that restful.

Anyway (as Jane would say), there probably aren't words for the pictures already forming in her precipitate mind's eye. Will the faceless numbered man to whom this letter is being sent (if, after reading it over and over, she has the courage actually to put it in a mailbox), will that man know anyway? Not very likely. Not unless he has an ear for the drumbeats that lie beneath words; and would a man with so acute an ear find himself in prison?

Of course, we don't know why he's in prison. Jane doesn't, either. What on earth has possessed her, a woman who is usually so cautious?

Well, what makes some words leap off a page or out of a song, instead of staying flat and more or less unremarkable? Something mysterious—hearts calling to hearts, or minds to minds, that sort of thing. Moments that override the usual, at any rate.

Normally, Jane wouldn't have seen that small advertisement deep in the Personals columns. She finds such ads depressing, and rarely looks at them. Most of them have to do either with groups eager to help people with this or that affliction, or with people in need of companionship, and neither kind is of interest to her. She has no particular afflictions (or at least none for the benefit of which any organization exists), and the companionship advertisements fill her with despair. What chance has she, when men and women of such capabilities and beauty, interests and gifts, must advertise for love? These are gods and goddesses, as they describe themselves, compared to her.

But here, right here, on this one-in-a-hundred day, were these few tiny lines that clamored and cried, leaping up and down for her attention. "Penpal for prisoner wanted. Man 'inside' wishes to correspond with woman on the 'outside' to share interests." What could be more innocuous, less eye-catching?

Oh Jane, you may be setting off on some adventure. The instant this letter is mailed, more events will begin to occur, and some of them will be out of your hands.

Never mind. Jane thinks she has merely been bent over her glass-topped coffee table, drinking tea and writing a letter that appears to have required writing. She could swear she had eloquence and fervor and beauty on the tip of her tongue, but none of that seems to have made the voyage through arms and fingers to the paper. She knows this letter does not contain what she contains, but what can she say?

If—when—he writes back, she might spill secrets, but it is, after all, an actual man who will receive this. She wouldn't care to sound like a fool, or like someone so hopeless she writes secrets to strangers.

She reads the letter over and over. Should she mail it? Well, she has to, doesn't she? There are these feelings and callings. Inevitabilities.

If there were no inevitabilities, how could Jane be who she is? She's hardly unique, of course; many people fall back on a belief in inevitability, and Jane is not so unusual.

She considers herself unusual, however, if not necessarily in appealing ways, and in that, as well, she is by no means alone.

This prisoner, also—he's unusual. Possibly unique. At any rate, he's certainly a statistical oddity, one of the relatively few who find themselves where he has found himself. Beyond that, he may be banal except for some criminal quirk. Or it may be that even his criminal quirk is banal. What is Jane's view?

Jane doesn't have a clear one. If she did, she would be terrified to send her letter.

She does have some idea, though, of what he isn't. He isn't scrawny or weedy, he isn't insignificant. He isn't sly. He is, in her mind's eye, a presence, anyway: full-bodied and blunt. Not the sort, say, to wear dirty white T-shirts, ribs and spare chest barely camouflaged, sleeves rolled up to contain cigarette packs.

But what has he done? Never mind his appearance, how about his character?

Jane could no more speculate on that directly than she could stare into the sun.

Her apartment is warm and stuffy, the small second-floor rooms drinking in heat all day while she's at her underpaid but air-conditioned library labors, and blasting it at her when she steps through the door in the evening. It isn't quite true, what she said in the letter, that the place is pretty well fixed up the way she wants it. There are dozens of things she wants to do to it yet, ways to make it pretty and welcoming. She is accomplishing this a little at a time, small projects for which she budgets. Next she will put new wallpaper in her bedroom. There are only three rooms, not counting the bathroom, but the brick house that contains them is stately and old and she feels some pride, entering or leaving. Perhaps passersby will think it belongs entirely to her.

There are women who could own a whole house like this one, but they're quite different from Jane. They would be, for one thing, rich; for another, astoundingly self-assured. Jane knows quite well the differences between that sort of woman and the kind, like herself, who rent upstairs apartments.

Downstairs, on the main floor, two men live together. She knows their names, and nods and smiles when she sees them, but oh, it makes her blush to think about them! Jane knows what things go on—it would be hard these days not to know about these matters—but to picture it, to *see* what must happen right beneath where she sleeps herself! It makes her stupid when she meets them downstairs and they're friendly—they would be friendly, after all—and what pops into her vision are oddly placed bodies doing amazingly intimate things to each other. She can't seem to prevent these pictures, despite embarrassment.

If she loved someone, and someone loved her, her body might also find itself in odd places doing amazingly intimate things. What freedom it would be, to be loved!

There is a mailbox down at the corner, and it's not awfully late yet. Perhaps the evening is cool. She folds the letter finally (it already has a number of creases, where she's been touching it, reading it over, and in the light of rereading, the words do begin to seem more interesting) and slips it into an envelope. Now she goes to the kitchen, where she keeps her stamps on a shelf over the stove. Not an especially good place to keep them in hot weather, over a stove. The glue doesn't hold, and she ends up taping the stamp to the envelope.

Won't that look peculiar, when it gets where it's going? Won't guards look suspiciously at a taped-down stamp? What could it be hiding—microfilm? Some drug? What kind of prison is it, anyway?

That's the sort of thing Jane no doubt ought to have checked before she wrote, much less set out to mail, her letter.

The two men from downstairs must be safely tucked away for the night. It's a fortunate thing that this house is so old and solid, because she almost never hears them, unless they're having one of their parties. They always take care to invite her, so of course she can't complain about noise, but she never attends. Imagine! Their parties would be no place for her.

Still, they do sound lively. And she wouldn't be alone, for she does hear women's voices sometimes.

Tonight, going down the stairs and past their door (with their names on a card beside it, bold as the brass apartment number) there is rock music playing. She would have thought opera or ballet.

How vulnerable she is to stereotype and cliché! Already she has two vague but quite dissimilar pictures of her letter's destination. One is of prisoners in some large and menacing mass, the way they show up on TV, rioting, holding hostages, escaping, being released to recommit horrible, unspeakable crimes. The other is of her prisoner alone: the man who wrote words that leaped off a page.

This is a quiet street of large brick houses overhung with aged maples. Still, Jane moves quickly. She isn't happy being out alone after dark. Such things can happen! They do happen, and seem utterly random: bogeymen lurking, watching for the helpless or the careless.

Even so she pauses, just for a moment, at the mailbox. One last look at the letter. One last qualm? Does she have some idea, then, of what she might be doing?

Apparently not. In the letter goes, through the swinging gate and out comes Jane's hand, empty. So it's done.

She walks home with a lighter step. She must feel she has accomplished something. And so, of course, she has.

A youth swoops past her on a skateboard, fluorescent shorts, long hair flying out beneath a headband. Wretched kids, frightening people, taking up the sidewalk.

Does Jane sound very old? She's only twenty-eight. If she has unfair images of the two men in the apartment below her, they might have unfair images of her as well. Here she is, single, twenty-eight, living alone in an adequate apartment, on a mediocre salary earned from an unexciting job. "Plain Jane," she used to be called on her worst days at school. Plain Jane she is still.

If she had her choice, she would be beautiful, or at least pretty. If she had her second choice, she would be ugly, because that would be dramatic also, in its way. Instead, inevitability has made her plain.

What could be done about this? She could dye her hair, but then she'd be a plain blonde person, or a plain red-haired one. She could have herself made over, perhaps, like those women in magazines, before and after pictures, always drab and unsmiling before, glamorous and radiant after. Imagine!

Or, of course, if she felt downright deformed (which she doesn't, really), she could have surgery. That seems simple these days, and all kinds of people try it. Indeed this thought has crossed Jane's mind. She may be looking in a magazine and see an entire face she'd like, the way other women may admire a haircut or a shade of lipstick.

Who would she be, though, if she didn't look like herself? The question stumps her. It worries her, the idea of learning to be someone else, after all this time.

Still, she has taken a step in that direction, with this letter she has mailed. (Which, by the way, she is already regretting, although it's the sort of relieved regret that goes with inevitability: there's nothing she can do about it now.)

Plain brown hair, plain straight nose (perhaps too sharp and narrow), plain pink mouth (a little thin-lipped, above a chin that's less firm and evident than it might be), plain blue eyes, plain brown eyebrows—she is trapped, apparently, between discontent with what she is and terror at becoming something else.

Again, not an extraordinary dilemma, although perhaps most people don't feel so fervently about mere appearances. Even the very beautiful may not think about their appearance as much as Jane considers hers.

She does wish, because she has a feeling this might make a difference, that she could discern just what plainness is. Taken one by one, her features are just ordinary, but taken together they become plain. What small effect is present, or absent, that makes so huge a difference? Jane has stared and stared into many mirrors.

Probably he won't write back. She thinks now that she hopes he doesn't, but surely she would be terribly disappointed.

She will watch the mail keenly every day from now on.

The downstairs apartment is silent when she goes past it this time, back up to her own place. What a haven this is, however hot—her own place.

In her living room she has white wicker furniture with fat cushions in various blue, green, and yellow pastels:

one chair, with footstool, and a loveseat. Loveseat! What can have possessed her? How much better to have bought a sofa, where she could lie full out to read or watch television, or knit, whatever. Loveseat! How the men in the furniture store must have laughed when she was gone.

Still, she has her hopes. She likes it, that her furniture is hopeful, also.

With a similar sweet optimism, she regularly buys cut flowers on her way home from work. In the early days of her job, of living in this city and in this apartment, she was somewhat embarrassed doing this: how clearly she was a woman who had to buy flowers for herself. Now, however, she has no trouble looking Mr. Alexander the florist in the eyes, and they smile at each other as he recommends something seasonal and inexpensive and wraps the blooms carefully, handing them over to her as if they were his gift. As flowers, in a good, fair world, are gifts from men to women.

Those currently in residence are irises: purple and silver and an astonishing golden yellow.

Jane's glass-topped coffee table would be perfect, not for writing letters to distant men, but for cheese trays, liqueur glasses, late-night mugs of chocolate. Floating marshmallows. This table is ready for any cozy moment (except for having to clear away the little heap of novels of historical romance, and the television guide. But that wouldn't take long).

There are switches for the old-fashioned (romantic) glass-globed lights in the living room and bedroom that will brighten and dim them, creating an atmosphere.

She might have been a Boy Scout, she is so prepared for eventualities. Anyone lost in this apartment she would lead to safety. She would lead, she is sure, to unimaginable, splendid heights and depths of pleasure, given the opportunity.

Meanwhile there are those huge and complicated novels in which the passion, however great, must be the mere shadow of her own, unleashed.

And now, too, she will have letters?

It's not so dull, after all, time spent waiting. There is plenty to occupy the mind, there are preparations to be made.

Jane wouldn't dream of hanging weeping clowns or velvet paintings on her walls. She has saved up for prints: the famous sunflowers, for one, and an impressionist field of undistinguishable mauve-blue-green. She aims for the soothing and avoids those aggressive female flowers that appear to her too grasping and voracious. She aims to seduce and hold with softness. The one who finally comes will sink into this place so far he won't be able to lift himself out.

Doesn't Jane sound predatory, though, a spider or a praying mantis of a female? But after all, what she hopes for isn't more than most people have. Why shouldn't she wake up in the morning, or go to bed at night, curled around another human body? Why shouldn't she have someone to welcome her home from work, or to talk with over breakfast? Why shouldn't she have someone else's furniture and art along with her own, some variety here? What reason on earth can there be that Jane shouldn't be loved?

Now she has taken to writing letters to strange, far-away, and possibly dangerous men. Well, who knows what will work?

Her bed is modern, simple white metal, with white matching metal bureau and white matching metal bedside tables, each with a small white-shaded lamp. There are pastel-patterned sheets and a billowing pink and gray duvet. It took months and months for her to save the money for all this.

She is decorating the set for a movie only she, so far, can see.

But don't think of Jane as pathetic; think of her as just as brave as she can be.

If she had a choice about it, her kitchen would be much bigger. As it is, although it has stove, refrigerator, dishwasher, it is small, lacking counter and cupboard space. There is no room for the elaborate food processor, the ice cream maker, the pots of flowering herbs, with which she would surround herself. There is no place, even, to sit down. In her mind a kitchen ought to be enormous, rows of cupboards, rows of hooks for hanging pots and plants, one long wall for a sofa, another for a huge stone fireplace. It ought to be possible to inhabit a kitchen. But people who live in apartments don't get kitchens like that. Perhaps nobody does any more.

The meals she would make! How delicate her dishes would be, cooked in the kitchen of her dreams and served up in the dim elegance of her living room. They would have to eat off the coffee table, she and her captivated companion, but there would be a candle or a flower in the center, and intricate bowls of Indian, Indonesian, Vietnamese, French—exotic, in other words—foods. Slightly pungent rice and balls of this and that rolled up in something else. Sweet sauces for dipping, and small glasses of spicy drinks. She would willingly spend hours in a kitchen on behalf of meals like that, for the purposes she has in mind.

For herself she may fry a chop, boil carrots and a potato. No desserts, except fruit or, very rarely, some treat like chocolates. It's not so easy, buying for one. A whole box of chocolates, for instance, would be too tempting, or would sit around for too long, spoiling, going dry.

We might say that Jane is like one of those chocolates, concerned with spoilage, her own dryness, but how predictable and trite! And anyway untrue, because that's not at all her concern. What absorbs her aren't losses, but the splendors of the gains she imagines she is missing.

She has a cup of tea before bed, curled on the loveseat in a pink nylon nightie. She is halfway through a long tale of courtly love, with handsome men of the aristocracy and beautiful and worthy (such an unfair combination!) women.

When was love invented, anyway? Does it make sense to be reading a book about love set centuries ago? She believes she has read that romantic love was actually invented, for some purpose or other, and people simply fell into the habit, with belief, relief, gratitude, joy, who knows? Maybe simply with obedience. Those were obedient times.

So are these. Jane is obedient, too. She longs to obey the rule of love. She wants in on the game: red rover, red rover, let Jane Smith come over— and crash, there she is, linking arms with the rest.

Her mind tonight wanders from the pages. What chance does courtly, historical love have, compared with her letter?

Also she has had, late at night for some years, a perfect companion. This is a man who, fortunately and for the most part, has no body or face or name. He is barely, in fact, a man at all, really mainly hands and a voice. He is, of course, a secret, and invisible, but here he is, real as real: his fingers, a hand, just touching her leg, resting now and then on her knee, otherwise stroking from her ankle up her calf, and above to mid-thigh, and back down. A tender caress, better than a hungry one: the almost taken-for-granted touch of someone so familiar he's simply here, reaching out but also absorbed in, say, his own book. So contentedly loving they would be, Jane and this man. How well her skin knows him!

This is nothing, really, to worry about, although sometimes she has worried anyway: say when she's downtown and has to step around some ragged woman in mumbling discourse with the unseen. These conversations tend, come to think of it, to be bitter, hostile, filled with grievance, whereas Jane's conversations with the unseen are tender, loving, often dependent on affectionate glances and gestures. Still, is there not a similarity? Might Jane, enjoying these quiet, private pleasures, not risk becoming too absorbed? Might those hands not take on more life of their own, following her into the street, into the library, resting themselves on her shoulders, or her hair, touching her in the small of the back or brushing across her breasts in public? She might very well turn to smile at such a touch, or incline slightly backward, leaning into phantom shoulders, even reach out her own hand to—nothing. Still very companionable, very loving; but from the viewpoint of the passerby on the sidewalk, or the library patron, or worse, her supervisor, Mrs. Curtis, what madness! Jane smiling at empty air, leaning back into vacancy, reaching out to nothing at all. Oh heavens, what if it went so far?

What if these moments began to occur outside and she didn't realize? Imagine Jane in twenty years, wandering the streets with an entire Cecil B. De Mille production playing invisibly around her.

For the time being, though, she anticipates those hands and that voice at odd moments during her days, the way a hungry person might anticipate a meal.

Still, tonight, as the hand rests on her here and there, she feels a disquieting difference, a wedge and a distance. It isn't enough.

It must all be in her head.

Ah, but that unknown prisoner, he has entered her head, is making himself known, making room for himself.

When will he get her letter, which day, what time, where will he be when it arrives? Will it be one of many, or all by itself? With what eagerness or hope will he open it? Will he smile, reading it, or toss it aside with contempt? Perhaps she should have scented it, to make it stand out. Or perhaps it will stand out more, being unscented and simple.

If he doesn't write back, what then? Actions can never be forgotten or undone (which is what makes action so terrifying). There'll be no ignoring that she wasn't satisfied, that she reached out with her pen for something else.

So maybe by now we're feeling more clever, more experienced and attractive, more—oh, let's say sophisticated—than Jane? Poor plain Jane, curled on her loveseat, reading her romance, her mind on warm hands, drinking her tea before bed—we feel a bit smug, do we, in comparison? With our absorbing jobs, after-work drinks, morning tennis games, vivid quarrels with lovers or mates, and vivid reconciliations? Going out to dinner, surrounded by friends, and viewing the latest films? Giving complicated, riotous parties in our homes, with all the fussing beforehand and the drowsy, hung-over cleaning up after? We probably have more in common with the men who live downstairs from Jane than we do with her. Our lives are in order, we know what we're doing, we've adjusted to what's possible and buckled down to it.

So maybe we're inclined to feel pity for Jane, or to worry about her, in a mildly superior sort of way? As if we have no secrets of our own. As if there's nothing we want so badly that it hurts to think about it.

It's not late when Jane goes to bed, putting down her book, falling asleep swiftly. She has to be up early to work tomorrow, just like most of us. Meanwhile, by her standards she's had a rather busy and eventful day, and needs her rest.

2

Jane's father, dead for a decade, was a man of few words, but the ones he did speak must have been powerful because they remain in Jane's memory, rolling out helpfully in his quiet voice when she needs guidance. "A fair day's work for a fair day's pay," for instance, comes in handy at those times she feels overburdened at the library; "What goes around, comes around" is like a rabbit's foot or a four-leafed clover, impelling her to good deeds on the understanding that some form of good fortune, or mere luck, will be returned to her.

He may have spoken in maxims and clichés, but maxims and clichés, she understands, are only rules that strike a chord of truth among their human hearers, and so persist.

"A healthy mind in a healthy body," her father said, urging her against taking up the unattractive and unhealthy habit of smoking. He never smoked himself, but nevertheless died relatively young, only in his early fifties, of a heart attack. Still, Jane's faith in the advice itself hasn't faltered.

So she has never even been tempted to smoke. Or to drink to excess, although of course there's nothing wrong with a glass or two of wine over a long evening in front of the television set. And she begins each day with a half-hour set of exercises.

To be truthful, though, all this stretching and bending has less to do with health than with appearance. To be truthful, Jane is tremendously pleased with her body, scrutinizing it mornings and evenings in the full-length mirror on the back of her bedroom closet door. With her strong, straight thighs, curved hips and high narrow waist flushing out to the fullest, warmest, most admirable of breasts, with all this, Jane is most content.

She loves, especially, her breasts. They're a handful, they are. Perfect pillows for troubled minds.

"You work with what you have," Jane's father used to say, and she works out every morning, working up a sweat, maintaining her virtues. None of her exercises are noisy ones, no running on the spot, for instance, because it's early and she wouldn't want to wake the men downstairs. She is a thoughtful neighbor.

Then, skin gleaming and hair damp, she showers. And this morning, here is her first picture of the day: that the prisoner, stocky, handsome, and free, might step into her bathroom and brush aside the shower curtain and be struck quite dumb. How could he resist reaching out? Oh, she shivers under his awed and tender touch, despite the water's heat.

She can hardly wait for whatever is going to happen. What an extraordinary shape her life is taking, she can feel it, she just knows. What an extraordinary shape that prisoner will have. In prison, people also exercise, there being not much else to do, no doubt.

All this is pleasingly vague. Her features, as she leans toward the bathroom mirror, foundation cream, then lipstick, then mascara brush in hand, are unpleasingly sharp. "Just put a bag over her head" is another cliché, although certainly not her father's. What an appalling point of view. She could weep at the words, and indeed tears do appear, threatening the mascara.

But why? She doesn't like her feelings getting this close to the surface of her skin.

Perhaps she's getting her period.

Unlike some working people, Jane won't rush her mornings. She drinks her coffee sitting down, reading a few pages of her book; none of this grabbing quick sips, snatching up clothes, and combing hair with an ear tuned to some morning TV program. She prefers a civilized beginning to her day, a few calm moments all her own.

Because after this anything might happen: she could stumble in front of a truck, or be taken hostage in a bank holdup, or be scolded by some unhappy library patron for something not her fault. These things happen to other people, after all, and there's no reason to believe her life is particularly charmed. People are taken hostage by one thing or another every day, there it is on her TV news, so why not her?

Not that she goes about terrified; just that she's aware.

On the other hand, she sent that letter last night, didn't she? And she has only the most optimistic, if blurry, pictures of how that must turn out.

Being alert has its limits, apparently.

Today Jane wears to work a straight gray skirt, white cotton blouse, plain white low-heeled shoes. It would be difficult to discern glamor or even shapeliness, but then, her longing is for a man who will see beneath surfaces. She wouldn't want to be misled (although could she not indulge, herself, in a little misleading? Something to

21

consider, but cautiously. "Beware the downhill, easy road," her father warned.)

Closing her apartment door regretfully behind her, turning the key in the deadbolt lock, she heads down the stairs once more to the world outside. The handrail on the stairs is old, and oak. In the small lobby opposite the apartment door of the two men, tin mailboxes are screwed side by side to the wall. It's stupid, but already Jane is glancing at hers, wondering about replies. Why, her letter is likely still in the box where she posted it last night, not even picked up yet, much less delivered, and here she is, already looking for an answer!

So easily and quickly a habit is begun.

The sun is shining again today, but there's less humidity. Of course, even though Jane's been up for so long, it's early, and the combined heaviness of heat and damp may still lower itself on the city. It's a two-block walk along Jane's dignified street to the bus stop, and a six-block ride from there to the library. Jane knows how to drive but sees no need for a car: it would be expensive, and working out parking arrangements seems to her more inconvenient than the inconveniences of not having a vehicle of her own. This isn't one of those enormous cities in which people travel miles and miles on expressways or in crowded trains. Often she walks to work, if there's time and if the weather is good. She prefers not to arrive perspiring, however, or drenched with rain or blown about by wind.

Today she might not even notice. Her gaze is turned inward, and she doesn't see the kids hurtling along the sidewalk in a game of tag, or the other passengers on the bus, or the driver, although as usual he greets her in a friendly way, as he does his regulars. Nor, unlike the princess and the pea, does she notice the rip in the maroon plastic seat she sits on. She often likes to watch the others on the bus, admiring a particular dress or the jut of a bearded jaw, or conjuring lives of more interest and glamor than her own, but today she stares out the window, seeing neither the streets nor the glare of sunshine, although she has left her dark glasses on the kitchen counter. If someone were going to take her hostage, this would be a good day to do it, because Jane might barely notice.

But what is she seeing? What events are occurring behind those freshly blue-shaded, brown-lashed eyelids?

Leaving the bus, heading the last steps to work, she even moves differently: as if she has recently left a perfect, most passionate lover and will be returning to him later. This way of walking, the way she feels, is just as real as real.

So it's odd, but not annoying (what could annoy Jane, feeling like this?), that she's going to have an ordinary busy day: arrangements to be made for visiting authors, an agenda to be typed for the next meeting of the library board, the front desk to be staffed for an hour, to cover for people at lunch. Jane used to believe a library was the very place for someone who enjoyed books, who, to be honest, even lived in them occasionally. It turns out, though, that real librarians have very little to do with books, but concern themselves largely with catalogues, orders, computers, and administration. They leave the more-or-less unskilled to deal with actual books, and the unskilled are too apt to be careless. But Jane doesn't mind, just for an hour, checking in returns, checking out new choices. It isn't awfully busy. She wonders if any of these people notice her particular glow today: her rosy, fleshy secret.

This secret is only that she's written a letter. Isn't there something just a little—ill—about the way it transforms her?

Jane works quickly, taking pleasure in efficiency. She believes people like Mrs. Curtis understand what a good worker she is, and appreciate it. If they see she has caught up with her own work, though, they may ask her to take on other jobs that aren't hers, like helping the young, frivolous, gossiping, careless girls return books to the shelves. Those girls tend to do the job helter-skelter, not caring that one author with an ordinary last name— Smith, say?—is different from another author with the same last name. They often don't try to alphabetize also by first names in these cases. Jane expects they make fun of the painstaking, slower way she works at the shelves. What makes the difference between her conscientiousness and their carelessness? It can't just be a matter of a few years. It must be a different way of viewing what's important. Or what is a person's responsibility.

"A fair day's work for a fair day's pay." But Jane might remember that she's not awfully well paid. And how does she make her fellow workers feel, these people who are not necessarily so very careless, just more light-hearted? She makes a virtue of single-mindedness, which to them may be no virtue at all.

Apparently they barely notice her. (But how can that be, on a day when she's so filled with this buoyant, unnameable pleasure?) Here she is, though, stooping at the shelves, among the Ds, and Sheila and Marcy, right over her head, are talking about dropping in at a bar after work. "Except I have to go home first and take care of things," says Marcy, young, oh young, and irredeemably perky. What could she have to "take care of"?

"Meet you there at seven, then," says Sheila. "I'll see if Liz and Alice want to go." But not, it seems, Jane.

She stands up so fast the blood rushes downward and she has to steady herself with a hand against a shelf. "You okay?" Marcy asks. "You're awfully white."

"Sticks and stones," Jane's father would have said. "Just sticks and stones, princess."

Still. "What about me?" she would like to cry. There's a song that says something like that.

"What about you? What do you mean?" they might very well ask. And it's not that she'd go; she's sure she would find an evening with them long and painful. She can imagine men coming to their table, luring her companions elsewhere, and soon she would be alone, unclaimed, smiling at nothing as if being alone were her preference, grasping and turning her glass to occupy her fingers.

Or she might get tipsy and loose-tongued, and tell them all about her prisoner.

She would like, though, to be invited. She'd like a chance to say something like, "Oh, I'd have enjoyed that. I wish you'd asked me earlier, but I can't, I'm afraid, I already have plans." Letting them know that she's quite busy with a life they know nothing about: many commitments, engagements, this and that.

Who would believe her? It's preferable, surely, to be ignored than to be a laughingstock.

No. No, it's not. Jane could learn to laugh, too. It's not that she can't see the ways she is ridiculous. She isn't crazy. Sane Jane, plain Jane—too many words rhyme.

She could be bold, she could say, "Seven o'clock? Fine, I can be there." Probably they wouldn't mind particularly, they'd just be startled. The words get as far as her throat.

The blood, returning to her head, turns her pink. And she sticks, she can't speak, and Sheila and Marcy move on to the next shelf.

Oh, Jane. Letter or no, new life or no, she is still traveling through her small world raw, missing a layer of skin. She is, like other fearful people, immensely irritating to be around. She has the air of a victim; and who wants to be close to that? Suppose it were catching? Suppose, spending time with Jane, others began to tremble also?

But it's true, she has a busy life after all: working on her apartment, holding down a job, reading books and watching television and, now, writing letters to a new acquaintance. Why, it's almost a full-time task keeping on the right side of reality, you can bet that's an interesting struggle all by itself.

"TGIF," the women at the library say. Thank God it's Friday. Jane picks up her purse, pushes open the huge wooden doors, and walks down the broad steps to the sidewalk, a little more weary than when she arrived this morning, feeling somewhat less blessed. But she is still someone with reasons to get home.

Not that there could be a letter yet. Where will her letter be now? Probably still only at the local sorting station. Oh hurry up, hurry up, postal workers! And be careful, don't let this be the letter that slips out of fingers and behind some counter, to be retrieved, if ever, months or years from now. Let that be someone else's letter, not Jane's.

She tries to calculate arrival times. Her letter would have been picked up today, it should be sorted tonight. Then, who knows? Since it's Friday, nothing will be delivered, perhaps nothing will even be moved, over the weekend. There may be some slender chance her letter will reach its address, a good three hundred miles away, on Monday. More likely Tuesday. Even then, there may be delays. Prisoners' mail must be censored. Not that hers says anything censorable, but it will still be read. (Something to keep in mind, for future letters. Assuming he answers.) Then there could be trouble over the taped-down stamp. And perhaps they (those in charge of prisons are already becoming "they" to Jane) don't trouble to take mail around to inmates promptly? Perhaps they hold it back as punishment, distribute it in bundles as reward?

Then if he does write back, that mystery man—mystery criminal—the process will have to occur in reverse, won't it? It could be weeks!

Don't let it be weeks. Already she can hardly wait.

She can't imagine what she hopes he'll say, in the letter he may or may not write. Something magic. Something more transforming than any beauty salon. Something more radical, even, than surgery.

It's really stupid for her to be disappointed that her only mail is a phone bill.

It's also stupid of her to open her apartment door and be, not merely disappointed, but almost shocked by its emptiness. What on earth was she expecting?

She sets out, paying precise attention to what she is doing, to toss a salad, fry a hamburger patty, warm a bun. Later she will have tea and read, maybe watch a little television. "Later" stretches before her like the Sahara, like Siberia, an after-dark tundra that doesn't bear thinking about. Although there is an unusual heat to this evening: a warmth drawing itself around a future she can feel, if not quite picture.

She thinks, "A fireplace, that's what I need." A wonder she hasn't thought of that before. Now she can feel herself and that companion, that man of letters, an arm around her, her head on a rock-solid shoulder, contentedly, sleepily watching a fire on an intimate Friday night. Just the two of them, watching on and on together.

Her body shifts on the loveseat, adjusting itself to his: flesh against flesh from shoulder to hip to thigh to foot. Oh my.

Then Saturday. "What goes around, comes around." Jane's weekends are not entirely her own. She has certain duties from which, presumably and eventually, some good will be returned to her, although it does seem sometimes that this is taking rather a long time.

For almost a year now, Jane has spent part of every Saturday on this investment in future good fortune, which also amounts, of course, to the general duty of a citizen to make a contribution of some kind. This is how Jane thinks of Lydia: as her payment and her social duty. Poor little Lydia.

And foolish Jane. How much more sensible for her to have sponsored some dark infant in a far-off country, whose gratitude could be presumed since it didn't actually have to be demonstrated. A controlled conversation between a benign, cheque-writing adult and a child whose life depended on her. That's what Jane should have done.

Instead, what did she do but sign up to be a big sister, committing three hours a week to a very tangible nine-year-old. It did sound appealing at the time, even a possible occasion of love.

Jane forgot that even as a child she wasn't all that fond of children, and they can still make her very nervous. Children seem to *know* too many things, they see too much. They can look at a person and feel their way precisely to whatever's in that person's heart. Although Jane can't recall having been wise in that way as a child herself.

Another thing about a foster child from overseas: it would have turned out a lot cheaper than Lydia, who has no shame about hitting Jane up for food, for toys—she must be costing Jane hundreds a year. "I got nothing for school," she says, looking up at Jane in a pleading, irritating way. Very likely it's true, but what requirements she has! Nothing secondhand, but thin designer jeans, little shirts with emblems. Jane had no idea, before Lydia, how expensive children's clothes can be.

She wouldn't spend so much on herself. Lydia can't get it through her head, apparently, that Jane isn't rich.

Well, to her Jane is rich.

Lydia, who is skinny, with flaming red hair and an odd and almost charming (except to Jane) aggressiveness, is going to be very beautiful, probably, in a few years.

Why should Jane go to the trouble and expense of outfitting a child who will grow up to be beautiful? Who will grow up to be the sort of woman who looks right through women like Jane?

What Jane really had in mind was a meek child, even a desperate one, whom she could expose to finer things: galleries, museums, books. "Look at this," she would have said, and "Here's a lovely book, I think you'll enjoy it." Aesthetic experiences for a hungry, possibly pathetic, mind.

"Oh, thank you," she pictured this child saying. And, some years down the road, "I don't know what would have become of me, if it hadn't been for you."

Silly Jane, who saw herself as a sort of Mother Teresa to the local unloved, or insufficiently loved, didn't dream of

29

a wiry Lydia who would complain, "I'm bored. There's nothing to do here. Let's go eat."

What a hungry child! Jane never seems able to get her filled up.

The little sister Jane had in mind wouldn't still be wandering around in her underwear when Jane, after a Saturday morning spent cleaning her own place, arrives at the awful red brick and concrete three-storey horror where Lydia and her mother, Lucy, live. "She'll just be a minute," Lucy tells Jane. "Why don't you sit down?" Lydia ought to have been out bouncing with anticipation on the sidewalk, watching for Jane to step off the bus, overflowing with pleasure and excitement and gratitude.

One thing Jane especially dislikes about picking up Lydia is the smell of this building: conflicting foods from conflicting stoves, dampness, perhaps, and the kinds of odors that build up when floors are never properly cleaned. Also something more, an unpleasant mustiness, the very smell of poverty and hopelessness, Jane thinks.

Jane would also think that since she isn't exactly a surprise guest, Lucy might take the trouble to be dressed when she arrives, but no, here's this lanky, dark-and-long-haired woman, not much older than Jane, still in her housecoat, making random attempts to houseclean, flicking a Kleenex over the coffee table, brushing crumbs off the couch. Jane feels that if she has the respect, herself, to dress smartly (today in beige cotton slacks, white blouse), Lucy could at least throw on some proper clothes to greet her.

(She doesn't wonder if it's not respect at all that makes her dress as smartly as she can manage; that it might be more a wish to show what they could do, if they had more gumption. They? Lydia, too? A nine-year-old? How harsh Jane is.)

What a foolish, light name Lucy has. No wonder she has such troubles, and needs a big sister for her child. How could someone named Lucy take herself seriously enough to cope? She can't, for instance, seem to balance her budget. Jane has even drawn up a budget for her, which is quite outside the responsibilities of big sister-hood, but still Lucy slips over into indigence by the end of the month. A week of waiting for the next mother's allowance cheque, with a package of hotdogs in the fridge and a box of corn flakes in the cupboard.

No wonder Lydia's so hungry. Jane does find it hard not to blame them, though. If people are in a circumstance, it's their job to find ways to survive in that circumstance.

"Where will you go for lunch today?" Lucy asks. She does try to be pleasant to Jane. What is it like for her every Saturday, seeing her daughter whisked away by this trim plain woman and returned with a full stomach and, often enough, arms full too, with toys and clothes?

"I don't know yet. I'll see what Lydia feels like." Jane wonders if Lucy should be invited along, at least some-times. Is there something wistful when she asks where they'll eat?

But Jane's job is girls, not women. She can't take on the task of feeding (or, horrors, clothing) entire families. "Somewhere not too expensive," she adds, feeling it neces-sary to make the point that she isn't made of money.

You don't *need* to be made of money to get along, that's what Jane believes. She thinks that if Lucy saved just a single dollar every week—and how hard could that be?—she'd have enough money in a few months to wallpaper this living room (as Jane plans to wallpaper her bedroom tomorrow). Not expensively, of course: she'd have to get seconds from a warehouse for ninety-nine cents a roll, but that would surely be better than living in this peeling beige hole. Nor can Lucy excuse herself by saying she only rents. Jane rents, too, and look what she's accomplished.

Lucy has enough money to buy her favorite women's magazine each month. What does she need with pictures of fashion and food, when she can't afford clothing and groceries?

Jane might think of how she looks, herself, at photos of beautiful women.

"Then," Jane says, "I think we'll just go to a park somewhere. Lydia seems to like that."

What Lydia seems to like is playing raucously with other children on the climbers and the teeter-totters. It's worrying, having to watch to make sure she isn't pushing or hitting or bullying another child for a turn at whatever it is she wants (especially if protective parents are nearby—there have been some near-confrontations, from which Jane felt saved only by the fact that she was most definitely not Lydia's mother, merely her temporary keeper). Still, playgrounds suit Lydia best. At least there she doesn't have to keep still. She can go on small rampages, getting things out of her system.

What Lydia needs to get out of her system is quite beyond Jane. Jane has no experience of fathers who rape, or of testifying in court, or for that matter of fathers who run away to avoid prison terms. No one knows where Lydia's father is—far away, anyway—and Lydia, reasonably enough, seems quite cheerful about not having a father any more. Jane doesn't have one either, but she still grieves. Hers was a kind man, and her childhood was, as she recalls, largely unrippled as far as he was concerned. Certainly unrippled compared to Lydia's. But Jane has emerged frightened from her relatively peaceful childhood, and

Lydia is coming fighting out of her violent and tragic one. Who can explain?

(Should it not occur to Jane that if Lydia's father hadn't jumped his bail, he'd be in prison? He might be a man running advertisements for penpals. He might be lonely behind bars, and longing for someone to whom he could justify himself. Like anyone else, Jane believes raping a child—any child, but especially your own, and especially many times—is unforgivably horrible. She would call that man worse than an animal—a slur on animals. Sometimes she looks at Lydia and goes blank wondering what the child has gone through. But not for a moment does she wonder just who she's sent her letter to. What's wrong with her? Is she dreaming of gentle bank robbers, compassionate killers, sweet lonely forgers and conmen?)

Lucy is a woman whose husband raped her child. And not just once. What on earth must that feel like? What was the moment like when she found out? How, for that matter, did she find out? How could she not have known, why was it a matter of finding out? How negligent she must be, a woman in a housecoat who didn't know her husband was raping her child.

On the other hand, she acted, didn't she? She turned on him decisively. She did, in fact, quite a huge thing, forcing him to the police, through the courts (until in some gross lapse he was allowed out on bail and vanished). Perhaps it was that huge act that wore her out, so she doesn't have the energy to get out of her housecoat today.

Jane has an uneasy feeling that she ought to be more sympathetic, but sometimes it's just too *hard,* knowing things. Some circumstances are altogether too real, and at the same time too remote.

Lydia, who is permitted to choose for herself what to put on, emerges from her bedroom in pink shorts (bought by Jane two weeks ago) and a white elasticized tank top. "Oh dear," says Jane, "I don't think you ought to wear *that*."

"Why not?" Lydia sounds merely curious, not defiant. Yet.

Well, why is because her small brown child nipples show through the stretched white top. Jane doesn't know how to say that. She doesn't know if Lydia is unaware, or if she wants to tantalize, or if, with all her ghastly experience, nipples don't mean to her what they mean to Jane. Could mean to Jane.

"If you wear shorts we might not be able to go everywhere we want to. And you might be cold if there's air-conditioning." She smiles. How wearing this is, and how grateful she is, after all, not to have to deal with a child every day.

Lydia shrugs and goes back to her room to change again. Now they're already twenty minutes into their three-hour visit. Jane has a keen sense of time about Saturday afternoons.

"Come on." Lydia, now wearing blue jeans and white cotton T-shirt (albeit with the screeching name of some band scrawled in green across the chest—whatever does a nine-year-old hear these days?), pulls at Jane's arm. "Ma's got company coming."

Was that Lucy's idea, to get them out fast? No doubt it's a man who's on his way. Maybe Lydia doesn't want to be around when he arrives. Maybe she's frightened. Perhaps Lucy has boyfriends in every Saturday afternoon, while Jane takes Lydia off her hands. Lucy is the sort of woman who probably wouldn't mind even if Lydia were home. Lucy would probably just take the man by the hand and lead him to the bedroom, and not even bother to close the door.

How can a woman whose husband raped her child have any faith in men?

It's amazing to Jane that while she and Lydia are setting out to pick their prickly way through the afternoon, Lucy is likely rolling around her untidy bedroom in the grip of lust and some hairy-armed man. A truck driver, construction worker, someone brawny and physical. Lucy would likely laugh at, say, an accountant. She wouldn't be able to take seriously a man who made his living solely with his brains.

Of course Jane spots no resemblance between the man she can see reaching his hands (short stubby fingers) between Lucy's legs, dipping his mouth to her breasts as he draws apart that easy bathrobe, shifting his body over Lucy's and beneath it and all around it—she sees no resemblance at all between the man who even now, at this moment, she is sure must be ravaging Lucy, and the man she has in mind.

If she looked more closely, she might see that their chests, their shoulders, their blunt toes, are very similar.

"Who's your mother expecting?" she asks Lydia as they head down the street to the bus stop. Jane prefers to linger as short a time as possible in this neighborhood: rude boys (rude girls for that matter) and rude adults, as well. It's menacing here, and foreign, like a country where she doesn't know the language and could offend at any moment, inadvertently.

"Her friend." Lydia doesn't look up.

"And who's her friend?" Really, Jane should be able to ask *some* questions, it's not as if she's being nosy. She does have some small relationship and responsibility to this pathetic family.

"Priscilla. I call her Prissy."

Well. This puts a new light on things. "I assumed she was expecting a man."

"No, just Prissy. They do each other's hair and talk a lot. She comes over just about every weekend."

"Do you like her?"

For once, Lydia's face shows something: light. "Oh yeah, she's neat. She was around when my father—you know." This is a child's voice, trailing off.

"So she helped then?"

"Yeah. She told my mom what we ought to do. She went to court with me, and I went to live with her for a little while after my dad ran away. In case he was mad."

If this Priscilla's so great, why did Lydia want a big sister in the first place? Maybe it was even Priscilla's idea, she sounds a little pushy. Imagine taking it on herself to tell Lucy and Lydia what they should do about Lydia's father! Of course something would have had to be done, but what a dangerous piece of meddling. Anything might have happened.

But then, anything already had. It's hard to suppose the situation could have gotten worse.

"Does your mother have boyfriends?"

Lydia glances up again, this time sharp and hostile. "What are you, our social worker?" She might be a truculent fifteen-year-old, not just nine.

"No, of course not. I just wondered."

"She doesn't have one now, but sometimes she does. It depends." On what? "Do you?"

Once, Jane took Lydia to the zoo, where the child showed an unhappy tendency to torment the animals, trying to toss pebbles and illicit food at them, or to poke them. Jane won't take her back there, but she recognizes the similarity, the way Lydia also likes to torment her.

36

Lydia must smell Jane's discomfort just the way she smelled the animals' unease.

For heaven's sake, she's only nine years old! Maybe she just wanted to get their attention.

"Do I what?"

"Have a boyfriend."

"I've told you before I don't."

"Oh yeah, I remember." Is that a sly look? "I just thought maybe you got one since." Well, why not? Other people gain (and lose) boyfriends in a matter of minutes, much less days. Anything can happen.

"There is someone I'm interested in, though," Jane says, "although he's not exactly my boyfriend yet." Dear God, why did she say that?

And having said it, doesn't she feel foolish! As if the words, spoken aloud, mock her precious, private vision.

"Yeah? Who is he?"

Good question. Jane hasn't the faintest idea.

"Just a guy."

Jane does wonder what Lydia's view of men can be; whether in this child's eyes, it might not be a wonderful thing to have no husband, and even no boyfriend. If being a virgin might not seem like a miraculous state, instead of merely freakish. A virgin would be somebody like Jane, but not like Lydia, who is only nine years old and hasn't been a virgin for years. What does Lucy, poor muddle-headed, disorganized, but once-ferocious Lucy tell her child about sex? Or, much harder, about love?

This might be something a big sister should tackle. But Jane's hardly an expert on the subject, either.

As usual, they have lunch in a fast-food restaurant packed with parents and children enduring each other or having a treat, but in any case noisy and messy. Jane has tried taking Lydia to proper restaurants, but Lydia can be a terrible embarrassment in places where manners are required. She's loud and she talks with her mouth full, and once, when Jane tried to correct her, she heard the child mutter, "Oh, fuck off." Imagine what might happen in an art gallery or museum.

Still, it's not a really bad three hours. Lydia entertains herself; she always has her eyes wide open for adventure, even if it involves falling off a climbing bar, which she does and then promptly picks herself up. She doesn't seem to need comforting.

Surely Jane doesn't envy Lydia, does she? Or Lucy? But at least things have happened to them. They appear to roll with their punches.

For Lydia's birthday three months away, Jane will knit her a sweater. She sees it pink, with pearl buttons down the front. It will be short, tight and gathered at the waist, loose and broad at the shoulders, an ample sweater made from soft, fine wool. If Jane can't figure out how to touch this child, at least she can knit. Also it will be respectable, a contribution to forming Lydia's taste. "Oh, is that ever pretty," she imagines Lydia saying, holding the finished sweater against her thin body, feeling its luxurious softness.

Jane keeps a keener-than-usual eye on Lydia at the playground, estimating measurements.

What sort of sweater would she make for her prisoner? Something bulky and beige, with a huge rolled collar and thick cuffs. (She hopes he's not the sort of man who'd want something garish, like ducks, on his chest. Not that she couldn't do it, just that those sorts of sweaters are so unattractive and so conspicuous.)

How beautiful he is. How thrilling, just knowing he exists. He puts a whole new light on things, even the sight of Lydia pushing dangerously high on the swings. How he might, if he were watching, admire Jane and her benevolence.

Lydia's jeans are dirty now, and Jane wonders vaguely what arrangements Lucy has for doing laundry. But children do get dirty, after all, and it's not Jane's problem.

Jane drops Lydia off at the front door of the apartment building. "Will your mother be home?"

"Oh yeah." Jane knows she ought to go up with Lydia and make sure. She ought not to leave the child unsupervised.

"I'll see you next week, then?" Jane is cheerful, since their next time together is now a whole week away.

She would have liked, very much, a little sister she could hug. She would have liked one who would have enjoyed hugging her, throwing her arms around Jane, arriving and leaving. But Lydia, too much touched, is quite untouchable. And how awkward and unmanageable it would be, if she collapsed against Jane and started to weep. What would Jane do about that?

Now, for the rest of the weekend, Jane really is alone. Heading home, she wonders if she may not be the only twenty-eight-year-old virgin in the world. (She blames this, too, on plainness, even though obviously millions of plain women are loved. She might do better to consider that there's nothing appealing or seductive about terror.)

In her heart, though, Jane is no virgin at all. In her heart she contains rivers of heat, avalanches of flesh, a whole earthly geography of desire.

Tomorrow the thirteen rolls of wallpaper propped in a corner will turn her plain white-painted bedroom into a festival of pink and silver flowers. Tomorrow, Jane has another full day planned.

And how many people can go to sleep hopeful almost every night, not even knowing quite what the hope is for? She wakes up hopeful, too. Match that, if you can.

And when this weekend is over, what excitement! By then, her letter truly will be out there somewhere, on the move, and all of a sudden her life will have such potential for surprise. No wonder that on Sunday she keeps finding herself smiling, even when it's really hard a couple of times to get the patterns to match on the wallpaper strips. She does think when she's finished, standing in the bedroom doorway, that it looks inviting. It should be sort of comforting, she thinks, especially to someone who's spent an unknown length of time in a small barren room, likely painted gray. She wishes she could tell him, right now, all the things he can look forward to.

3

"You're looking well, Jane," Mrs. Curtis says in a tone of some surprise. It's true that Jane's skin is more flushed, and even seems to have drawn itself more tightly over her cheekbones.

"Thank you." Jane glances down. She doesn't like to be scrutinized, but she is pleased. She feels well.

She is feeling—oh, restless, eager.

The prisoner is filling out nicely. He still has no face, but she can now see the individual hairs (light brown) on his arms. There are a few freckles on his back. When he stretches, the muscles of his thighs will stir and jut. His calves will be taut, his ankle bones protruding. His hip-bones also. He has a waist that's narrow, relative to his broad chest and his wide shoulders. The palms of his hands have deep lines (which she will be able to feel on her breasts when he touches her). They also will be the hands of a worker, with, if not exactly calluses, a certain rough-ness. Well-used hands.

What leap of vision brings his hands anywhere near her breasts? What has possessed her, that virtually overnight these adjustments, advances, can occur?

It seems quite natural now that he is in her life, pre-pared at a moment's notice to admire or embrace her.

Does he make license plates in prison? Does he sweat in the laundry, peel potatoes in the kitchen? Does he work out in the gym or do exercises in his cell? What sort of profession did he have before he went to prison? Did he work at all?

Jane doesn't care. What she cares about is this entirely new and astonishing life he so miraculously provides her. While she waits, of course.

In supermarket checkout lines, she scans the headlines of lives far more dramatic than hers, but isn't envious. Who would be an eight-year-old giving birth to twins, or even a movie star trapped in a large color photograph with some young woman not his wife, for all the world to see? How humiliatingly public.

Here's a sort of Zen question: Does embarrassment exist if there's no one around to see it? Jane does wonder.

Once when she was young, barely a teenager, maybe fifteen years ago, she overheard her mother on the phone, laughing with a friend. "Well, you know," she was saying, "my poor plain Jane." In reference to what? It doesn't matter—the point is, that was her own mother.

"You need," her mother also said, "to get out of yourself more, Jane. Why don't you join some clubs at school?" Well, maybe she was worried, maybe that was her way of saying, "I want more for you, because I love you." Who knows? The lives of mothers and daughters are filled with mishearings and misinterpretations, after all. What Jane heard was, "You aren't good enough, big enough, *enough* enough."

Her mother is a sociable sort, herself. Of course she has had advantages denied to Jane.

How was it when Jane was born? How long did the labor go on, and how much pain was involved? Where was her father? Did her mother cry out, or was she unconscious, knocked out by drugs, when Jane finally emerged, all pink and slippery? When she saw Jane that first time, probably cleaned up by then and wrapped in a blanket in the arms of a nurse, what was her first thought? Might she have wept for joy, or for sorrow, or, worst of all, for pity? Did she think, "Oh, how beautiful, how perfect," or, "What a shame she's so plain."

All babies are plain. At best they are plain.

What about her father? He was the sentimental one. Her mother was merely lovely; glamorous, even, in a small-town way. And she kept, keeps, herself well: hair done every two weeks, maintained in a short upswept style and perfectly blonde. Her regular, yes, pretty, features are improved by expert makeup over good bones. And always blood-crimson nailpolish, perfectly applied and perfectly, regularly, removed, no chipping or flaws. Jane can recall being raked, not seriously and certainly not deliberately, by her mother's fingernails. How ever did the woman change diapers?

When did she find time for so much care? And how could she be sure she wasn't just making a fool of herself?

It was Jane's luck to take after her father. Not that he was bad-looking, but standards are different for men. If Jane had been a boy, her life would have been entirely different.

How could Jane's mother, with her crimson nails and lipstick, her glossy hair, her wide-spaced blue eyes, her perfect cheekbones and perfect straight and narrow nose— how could she begin to know how it was to be Jane?

Imagination ought to be a requirement for mothers. It ought to be expected that they will be able to place themselves in their offsprings' little sneakers.

It's not that Jane dislikes her mother. You can't dislike someone for being beautiful, can you? Only, so much seems to go along with beauty: certain assumptions of ease. And it's not that her mother didn't try. When Jane was little, her mother took the child along with her to her own hairdresser every couple of months, with pictures clipped from magazines. Jane could never see a resemblance between those photographed children and herself, but nevertheless, some weeks her hair was crimped and curled, other weeks long and (very temporarily) waved. They must have tried everything. Jane, watching herself in the mirror under the harsh salon lights, understood that her mother must consider all this a necessary investment, simply to maintain Jane on the tidy side of humanness.

They see little of each other any more. Obligatory occasions such as Christmas, mainly. There are lines around her mother's mouth and eyes, and small crinklings in her skin, but she really hasn't changed that much.

When Jane turned twelve, her mother subscribed to a couple of magazines for her. Page after page of beautiful, cute, pretty, lissome, nubile—all those words—girls. Evidently these were what her mother had in mind.

No wonder Jane doesn't like to be looked at too closely.

Still, these days she can imagine parts of her own life made public. Here she is, walking gracefully, blissfully, toward television cameras, holding hands with her prisoner, for a program on love. "This is the story," says the narrator's low and mellow voice, to the accompaniment of, say, gentle music played on a flute, "of a most unlikely love affair. It is about two unusual people living quite different lives far apart from each other, who came together in a magic way. And these two people have created

44

together what some would call an ideal love: a noble alliance of the mind and heart and body."

Well, perhaps that's a bit much, even for Jane; the script may need work. Nevertheless, the commentator would speak of their histories, hers and her companion's, the virtues of the sturdy love of a good woman, her prisoner's newfound gentleness, and the radiance of her confidence (which would not be known to be also newfound).

She would tell about how she saw that advertisement and simply knew. She could talk about her leap of faith, her certainty. "I never had a moment's doubt," she'd say, and smile.

He would say, "There was something about her letter, out of all the ones I got. It just leaped out at me. It was like I knew this was my future." He'd smile, too. They'd smile at each other, and squeeze hands.

Okay, maybe it still needs work. But that would be the basis of it. Jane finds herself walking along the street with her hand turned slightly outward, as if it's being held, moving slowly as if she is stepping toward cameras. Whatever must she look like!

She has nothing to wear. Nothing at all suitable for public appearances, much less for greeting him. Her most stylish and presentable outfits are nightgowns, chosen to dip to her breasts and follow the lines of her hips and cling to her legs. The matching robes would fall from her shoulders in a moment, at the touch of a pair of hands. Any one of them would easily slip up, at a touch, beyond her calves, her thighs, just the way they do in books, on television.

Her prisoner, though, would exist in the morning as well as the evening, seeing her off to work and greeting her on her return. (He is unemployed, then? Apparently so. At least she sees him always in her apartment.) Her sensible dresses and practical coats are not the thing at all for tender, lingering moments at the door. She has been willing (if reluctant) to buy new fashionable clothes for Lydia, but why should Lydia's need be greater than her own?

She needs, she sees, looking into her closet, everything. This is what preparing to shoot a movie must be like: designing just the right look to reflect the characters and plot, down to the smallest detail. Not just the dresses and slacks and blouses and jackets, but the shoes and the stockings, belts and scarves. Where to begin?

And when? Say she went shopping after work, that would be the very day a letter would be waiting. She is so eager, at the end of the day, to get home!

So far, nothing. But that daily disappointment also means daily anticipation. It evens out, so far.

She can hardly use her Lydia hours to shop. That wouldn't be fair to an impatient child; but also, Lydia wouldn't share her tastes, would urge her into tight bright sweaters and bold high-heeled shoes. Jane wants to look interesting and appealing, but she has no intention of looking like a tramp. She wouldn't want to resemble Lucy in any way.

The world is full of Lucys. What if her prisoner were tempted by women like that?

Unkind Jane—she's never even seen Lucy with a man, except in her own head.

She has no idea what to buy.

She chooses a Saturday morning (no mail, and before Lydia), dressing carefully in white blouse, blue skirt, easy things to change in and out of. She can see this is precisely the sort of outfit to avoid. Today she must shop with an eye on desirability, from the point of view of her prisoner. It is necessary to keep in mind the details of their life together.

So she buys, for one thing, tight but soft blue jeans, and pastel T-shirts, for those weekend mornings they will work together cleaning her apartment. He will be diverted by his view of her bending, washing the floor or putting a pot away in a low kitchen cupboard. She feels him gazing at her, reaching his hands out to her hips. This will make cleaning the apartment a good deal more entertaining than in the past. Or in the present, for that matter.

For work—well, there is some climbing involved, and stooping, as well as sitting at her desk. But what a difference it makes to wear delicately patterned suits, with sleek tops that follow the lines of her breasts, tuck in at the waist and flare out at the hips, with skirts that have promise. By promise, she means that while they are not tight, and do fall below her knees, they are of pale blues, greens, rose, soft shades hinting at other softnesses.

What kind of woman wouldn't have realized long ago that clothing is symbolic, that it refers, discreetly and silently, to something its wearer wants to make known?

But then, she did know that, in a way. It's just that her message has changed.

Very high-heeled shoes are out of the question—how could she walk even as far as the bus stop, much less stand at her job or in bank and supermarket lines?—but what a world, again, of colors! She has worn black or beige or white pumps, plain, in the past, but now finds herself reaching out toward open toes, slingbacks, in blues and pinks, and toward sneakers that make her feet want to leap and run. Who knew before what joy there is in footwear?

And why wear only beige stockings? Try black and silver and patterns, why not?

She has trouble, hurrying home, carrying all her packages. There's no time to linger over what she's bought; she has to hurry out again to get to Lydia's.

When the time comes, she'll have to turn Lydia over to some other big sister. There are far more pleasurable prospects for those three precious weekend hours. The thought of being rid of the burden of Lydia, for reasons the child will surely have to understand, makes Jane feel light and free.

The anticipation makes her patient with Lydia, kinder and even generous. "Look, Jane," and the child pulls on her hand as they pass a store, "isn't that neat? Can we look at it? Please?" "That" is an odd, sloppy outfit: loose garish shorts with a violently red top that picks up one main color in the shorts.

"We can look." Jane knows, though, that she will end up buying it for Lydia, if that's what the child wants. What does it matter, when she's already spent so much today? And perhaps it will count: adding to her score of virtue, adding to her enormous, accumulated reward.

The outfit does look strangely appealing on Lydia, although Jane wouldn't have guessed it would. Wearing it, Lydia looks almost vulnerable, muted in comparison with its vividness. There's something brave about those thin, sturdy legs. Just for a moment, Jane rests her hand on Lydia's head.

It's much easier to be kind, knowing there's an end in sight. Jane thinks that perhaps she's been taken over by the inevitable tenderness of saying good-bye, even though of course it's not yet time for that.

"Thanks," is all Lydia says. Jane wonders if Lucy will like the shorts and top. Will their colors run in the wash, making her life more difficult?

Too late to worry about that now.

Jane looks pleasing too, when, alone later, she tries on her new clothes in front of her mirror, bending and pirouetting and smiling.

But what if people look at her, all newly outfitted, and see that whatever they assumed, she has been unsatisfied but now has hopes? They'll see that there's something she wants. Her past may become more pathetic to them, her future more pitiable. What could be more amusing than knowing that someone has hopes? How they might laugh!

Even Jane has some difficulty looking herself in the eye.

Still. Her legs—how shapely they are, how hard to believe that they aren't irresistible, that there aren't hundreds of eyes admiring them and hands desiring to touch them. That narrow waist, those promising tips of hip-bones, the flourish of ribs toward those flourishing breasts—Jane is so pleased she does a little dance on the pink bedroom scatter rug.

On Monday she will wear her new pale blue seersuckerish suit, with the narrow white vertical lines, and the pale blue sandals with the narrow, low heels. The suit jacket, shrugged open or off, will display a crisp but soft white blouse.

All this has been more expensive than she would have dreamed, and it will take her some time to pay it off. Will someone in the credit card office (which she imagines filled with rows and rows of desks, rows and rows of computers, rows and rows of workers, mainly women) pick out her bill and notice she's been on a spree? Will the woman call out to a colleague something like, "Look at this—that Jane Smith sure has bought herself a lot of stuff. Something must be happening to her, I wonder what?" Would they be able to make a picture of Jane and her longings, from the items on her Visa bill?

What should she do with her hair that would suit her new clothes? Some easy style that can survive her passionate new life. Not as simple a style as her mother's, though, and not blonde like hers, either. That kind of simplicity requires fine features and good bones.

It would be sinful, of course, to think that the wrong parent died. But she does believe her father loved her; certainly he never made a sign that she wasn't just fine with him. He called her "princess," and then he had his heart attack and died when Jane was just eighteen. Oh, she howled and wept then, putting her mother to shame with her grief. "Jane, if you can't keep yourself under control," her mother said, holding herself up straight and somehow tight, "I think you'd better stay home from the funeral. You can't carry on like this in public." Even Jane was surprised by the wildness of her grief.

Her mother marched off like a soldier, to bury her husband. Home afterward, still stiff and dry-eyed, she handed out sandwiches and cakes and cups of tea to the other mourners. Jane was appalled, later, to hear her weeping in the darkness, in the room she'd shared with Jane's father. What gave her, with her matching lipstick and nailpolish in place even on this day, the right to weep? What did she have to cry for?

It was hard to imagine they had much of a life together, besides their common interest, Jane.

Well, it was time for Jane to think of leaving anyway, then. Was she braver ten years ago than she is now? Or was it just another instance of inevitability and necessity? At any rate, she sent out letters and résumés, making herself sound as good on paper as she could manage. Thank heaven she knew how to type: her only saleable skill, apparently, in a world that did not give much credit to adequate marks in English or history or even math. She could have gotten work in a life insurance office, or a car rental outlet, or even a travel agency, she applied for all those. What came through, though, was the library.

"I'm leaving," she told her mother, not without triumph although what did she think she was triumphing over?). "I've got a job away. All I have to do is find an apartment for myself."

Was her mother startled? Sorry? Jane couldn't tell. "Very good, dear," she said. "It sounds the sort of thing you'll enjoy. And of course it's time to be out on your own. I've always known you couldn't stay here forever."

Well, how was Jane supposed to interpret those words? They couldn't have been much more ambiguous. She heard relief: that her mother was now free, of daughter as well as husband. Or did her mother also weep, alone not merely in her room but in the entire house, on the night of the day Jane left home?

Her mother has friends. They play bridge or go to movies or just sit around one of their living rooms some evenings and drink wine, eat cheese, and chat. It does give Jane a little pleasure, she thinks, that her mother must have so little to boast about when those women start comparing offspring. "Oh yes, well, Jane, you know," she hears her saying, "she's still at the library. Doing quite well, I believe, but still there."

For all Jane knows, those women are just like her mother. Maybe they're too absorbed in their own lives

51

even to mention daughters and sons. As long as their children are gone, maybe that's all that really matters.

Her mother has even gone out with men since becoming a widow. Perhaps that's reasonable—her husband's been dead for a decade, after all—but as far as Jane's concerned, it's as large a betrayal, as great a faithlessness, as if he were still alive.

Jane has met only one of those men, Mel, who dropped in on one of Jane's rare visits home—her birthday? Her mother's? Anyway, a big man, Mel, well into his sixties, wearing light blue pants and a red plaid shirt, with a blue tie, white shoes, blue socks—oh dear! He spoke in a loud voice and made Jane's mother laugh and flush. She fetched him beer from the fridge. Jane's father had been a quiet man, his clothes were subdued, he drank, but only rarely, rye and ginger ale. How could she?

If Jane had not been there, would the two of them have kissed, embraced, headed eventually for her mother's (and father's) bedroom, to touch each other with Mel's plump hands, her mother's lurid fingers? Jane could hardly bear to speak to him, and sat curled in her chair, her body slanted away from him. When he left, her mother scolded her for rudeness. "He was my guest," she said, "and you're in my home." As if Jane were a stranger. As if the home belonged only to her mother, was not bought with her father's years of labor.

How could a woman well into her fifties still have lovers? And she'd already had a husband. It seemed to Jane, still seems, that there are too many of these greedy women in the world, devouring far more than their own share of men, leaving none for the starving, like Jane.

The house is all different now. Her father's possessions—the collection of knives that hung on the living-room wall, the photo of his parents, even the tweedy brown easy chair he liked to sit in—have disappeared. Her mother bought a couple of framed landscape prints, fields and farmhouses, and got herself a burgundy lounge chair of the kind that unfolds, a stool appearing for the feet. She bought a new television, too, and now has a video cassette recorder. Maybe she and her friends rent dirty movies, watching them, giggling, during their wine and cheese nights?

She has put away the family pictures: those small framed snapshots of holidays when the three of them were all together. Jane's father, not usually bold, would approach total strangers and hand them his camera, so that he could be in the pictures with her mother and herself. They went every year to visit shrines, old forts, and crowded beaches. Did they have a good time? Jane's recollections are unclear.

Her mother has had sprightly wallpaper and light-colored paint applied in all the rooms. There isn't even a familiar smell left, it's all been covered over, camouflaged.

Jane has her own home. Her new bedroom wallpaper makes her feel as if she now sleeps in a garden. And she has a lot to look forward to, besides.

Right about now, wouldn't we just like to grab Jane and give her a good shake? "For goodness' sake," we might say, teeth gritted, "do stop. There's nothing more unattractive than whining, even to yourself. People are beautiful in different ways, you know. It's who you are that counts. Looks have nothing to do with it." And other, similar, buck-up suggestions. But don't expect a plain person, even a more successful one than Jane, to believe a word.

The fact is, plainness does count. There's even been research on the subject. Plain people are assumed to be duller than the lovely. Teachers spend less time with them. More attractive people than plain ones go to university. An attractive person is far more likely to be hired than a plain one. Even parents are more apt to embrace a pretty child.

It may be perfectly true that a plain person can be magnificent in some way, and there is no reason a plain person won't be loved by someone, but what determination it may require, what overcoming of the odds! Show Jane where, on television or in her books, there are plain women who could prove the point to her.

Her name *is* unfortunate. If she'd been called Sarah or Bonnie, no one on a school playground would have thought to call out "Plain Sarah" or "Plain Bonnie," but a "Plain Jane" was irresistible. Imagine standing in a schoolyard at recess being called Plain Jane by children who, being children, were delighted by their wit.

But then, too, look at what other plain people have done with their lives. Jane, catching sight of Janis Joplin's face on an album cover in a record store one day, was amazed by a wild-haired woman even plainer than herself. Home, she listened to that raucous, soaring voice and stared at the photograph and believed that if she had the gift, she might pour it out like Janis Joplin, making people feel the pain down to their bones.

Janis Joplin had lovers: many of them, and of both sexes. Well, that may be going too far beyond Jane's imaginings (or desires), but how she admires the forthrightness! Joplin must have just gone out and grabbed people to love or to comfort her.

Southern Comfort, that's what she drank, isn't it?

What if Jane could just go up to likely-looking men and say, "Come home with me. Let's see what happens. Mightn't it be fun?" Well, mightn't it?

But it would have been different for Janis Joplin. She was brilliant, and brilliance is a powerful attraction, even sometimes to men. And even Janis Joplin, a successful plain person, died unhappily young.

Jane looks and looks each day, going and coming, for the letter in the mailbox. Other events these days feel somewhat—misty. Sometimes at work it's hard to take in people's words, although she does hear when Mrs. Curtis says, "You're looking well, Jane," in that slightly surprised way. Outdoors, the sunshine, trees, and grass, even the air, touch her only lightly. All this feels somewhat movie-ish: perhaps an old romantic Hollywood film, shot through gauze or Vaseline; or, more ominously, a north-ern-lit Bergman.

Sometimes Jane feels touched, just lightly on the shoul-der, by some divine finger. Remarkable.

How loved she is: by a man who sends her smiling into the world each morning and greets her with an embrace each evening. She turns to him on the pillow beside her every night. These nights she goes to bed much earlier than she used to, not to sleep but to feel the sweet warmth of her companion. She is hardly ever lonely these days and nights.

They don't need to speak; conversation is hardly the point. (A good thing, too, since Jane has no idea what they'd find to talk about, or what they'd have in common.)

He still has no face, but otherwise continues to fill out nicely. He is now barrel-bodied, bold, and (to Jane) pro-tective, a man with, not long arms, but quite strong ones. He has sturdy thighs and blunt toes. He is slightly older than Jane (and wiser? smarter?) so the curling hairs on his chest are salt and pepper, and profuse. No hair on his back, though, or his shoulders, she has specific tastes. He is less gentle than her now-absent companion hand, but never brutal.

He would understand how it is, being trapped inside something, waiting, a prisoner himself.

Meanwhile, she hurries to make her apartment perfect, putting a fresh coat of ivory paint on her kitchen, and wallpapering a bluebell border. When carpet cleaners phone one evening, she agrees to have them do the cushions of her furniture. What a surprise for them, reaching someone who says eagerly, "Oh yes, please. How soon can you come?"

The cleaning men are unimpressive: thin and stupid. What a contrast to her prisoner! Oh, Jane does feel a lucky woman.

Until quite recently, she might have considered them more carefully. Of course, until quite recently she wouldn't have wanted her cushions cleaned.

On a Saturday morning she walks the four blocks to the florist's with a view to picking out something both more permanent and more dramatic than cut flowers. Mr. Alexander will help her choose the right thing and advise her how to care for it. But instead of Mr. Alexander, there's a teenaged kid in charge. "Is he not in on Saturdays?" she asks.

"Yeah, usually." The boy she thought at first looked sullen actually looks sullen and sorrowful, she sees. "He got beat up Thursday night. He was taking money to the bank and somebody hit him on the head. He's in the hospital."

"Oh no! Is he badly hurt? Will he be all right?" Jane can feel all her own night terrors, the randomness of tragedy. She could have told Mr. Alexander he shouldn't go wandering around carrying cash at any hour of the day, much less at night.

"They think so. He's got a fractured skull, so they're keeping him in for a while."

"You're just filling in?"

"He's my grandfather. We're taking turns in the family. He was worried about the store being closed, losing business."

That's nice. That's what a family should be like, taking care of each other. They must think a lot of him. Poor man, being struck down for his money. It wouldn't likely have been much. Who would do such a thing?

"Have they caught who did it?"

"Oh yeah, right away. A couple of people saw what happened and called the cops, and they chased the guy and got him. I guess he's done it before. The cops say this time he'll be going away for a while. I'd like to get my hands on him first, though. Me and my brothers." He's not a big kid, but he looks angry enough.

She buys a large brass planter with a large green plant. "I don't know, I think there's instructions here someplace for it," he says, rooting through a desk drawer. "Just give it some light and water, I guess."

Later she also buys a small ceramic-tile cheese tray, which comes with its own small sharp knife. And she invests in a white lace tablecloth, although not a large one, since she has no dining table. It will transform her coffee table, though, for more formal occasions.

She hopes the prisoner isn't clumsy, won't spill anything, say, red wine or spaghetti sauce, across it. But of course he will be graceful. Strong and powerful, but graceful.

And good. Reformed. Not a mugger. Nothing like that.

Always her eye, morning and evening, goes to that mailbox in the entranceway downstairs. Sometimes, before she goes to bed, she even goes back down for a final look, although of course mail never comes in the evenings. But just to be sure, just in case she missed the letter earlier.

Now and then she does get just a little annoyed. Who does this man think he is, not writing? It's been three weeks, and what else does he have to do but sit in his cell writing letters?

Apparently he doesn't know they have a life together now, he and Jane.

She is some distance ahead of him in all this.

How does he spend his days? Her pictures of prison are from films: rows of barred cells, tiers of them, one above the other, a lot of noise and constant threats of violence. Guards who may be more desperate and cruel than the men they are responsible for restraining. He'd have such amazing stories to tell her, events and circumstances far outside her knowledge.

She watches other men, catching glimpses of him. And ruling out some parts of them. No baldness, for instance, no red hair, no bellies popping out over belts. (Her standards of appearance are a good deal higher than the ones she wishes men would have, aren't they?)

These men she scrutinizes, what are their suits, jeans, T-shirts, shorts, ties, jackets, socks—all that camouflage they wear—what are they covering? Long tanned limbs; thin hairy white ones; broad chests or concave ones; wide shoulders or scrawny ones. Massive—things—and puny ones. What kind would be best for her: something large and possibly painful, or narrower, more slender, more tender, perhaps?

Do men's things match the rest of them? Does narrow go with narrow, thick with thick?

A man would be awfully startled to find himself in her life, wouldn't he, discovering how little she knows? Perhaps a prisoner would be too hungry to notice.

What would he read, what sort of books? What if he liked only Westerns, or war books? What, even worse, if he were actually illiterate? Many criminals are. That's believed to be one reason they become criminals, because they can't read and there's no place in the world for men who can't read.

Well, she could teach him, couldn't she?

If he would only write to her. If he wrote, she could write back, and ask him what he likes to read. Because, how stupid, of course he's not illiterate, or he wouldn't have been able to write his advertisement in the first place, or read any of the replies.

How many replies has he received? Even on paper, Jane may have given a dull impression.

Would she dare to ask him for a photograph? No. Then he might do the same.

She dresses in the morning hoping he would like this outfit. She undresses at night hoping he would find her tempting. She goes through the day feeling his eyes on her.

Now and then she remembers that she doesn't even know his name and has, in her thoughts, nothing to call him.

She wonders whether he might find her apartment, so carefully decorated, a little unnerving, whether he would be uncomfortable, settling his big firm body into wicker, or might prefer a sturdy dark wood bed to white-painted metal, or walls that are less pastel. Surely, though, he must long for softness and color. Surely any prisoner would find her apartment a relief.

After a cell, wouldn't he just sink in here and never venture out again?

She feels herself floating on desire in much the way that Jesus walked on water.

Saturdays are tough: no possibility of mail, combined with the necessity of Lydia. There's no floating dreamily through an afternoon with her, although they manage.

Sunday is worst: long and eventless, except for the anticipation of tomorrow, Monday, any weekday for that matter, when it is possible she'll come through the door from work and there will be a plain white envelope showing through the mailbox slits.

Oh please, faraway prisoner, don't have received Jane's letter and torn it open and just skimmed the words over which she did labor in her way, tossing it aside. Don't have decided there's no promise here.

Did she make herself clear? If so, might he not have dismissed her words as lightly, as easily, as thoughtlessly as, let's face it, he'd dismiss Jane if he met her at a party. (How would he meet her at a party? Jane doesn't go to parties, and he can't.)

What is he doing, what is he doing right this minute, while Jane lies awake in her white metal bed all alone with a head full of dreams?

Perhaps he is asleep.

4

"Dear Jane Smith," it begins. How ordinary. How extraordinary.

She has been waiting for weeks for the click of the letterbox in the entranceway downstairs, but of course when it comes, she is at work. For hours the envelope sits there, with only the letter carrier aware of its arrival, and he would neither know nor care how, even before it was written, this letter has shifted Jane's life.

When Jane comes through the door tonight, her eye racing first thing to the slit in the silvery mailbox, she has to reach out and steady herself against the wall, she feels so odd and light-headed. Her fingers tremble, unlocking the box with the tiny key she keeps on her key ring.

The return address of the penitentiary is stamped on the upper lefthand corner. Her own name, her own address, are written across the center. She peers, still standing at the bottom of the staircase, at the handwriting: what does it say? A careless, hurried scrawl, one of many letters sent? Or large and firm, like the man himself in Jane's view?

Jane is wearing yellow of various shades of sunshine today: a vivid wraparound skirt, quite smart, that flares slightly open as she walks, revealing knees and hinting at thighs; and the palest of pale blouses, skin like the moon showing through.

Her stockings are sheer, her pumps a light blue. Also light blue is the scarf tied in such a nonchalant, carefree manner around her throat that she could be someone flamboyant, an Isadora Duncan of the bookshelf. (Keeping in mind it was a scarf that did in Isadora Duncan.)

She thought her scarf was flamboyant? Look at the great loops of these letters spelling out her name, her street; look at the way they run, race, almost off the end of the envelope, as if what he was writing was too big to be contained. How sure of himself he must be, to write like this.

What is he sure of, exactly?

This is magic, this letter with its queen's-head stamp, its blue-printed return address, its deep black ink. It's startling that she hasn't, in some way, expected this; that the real thing has come, as it so often does, as a surprise.

A bit unnerving, really.

She would have thought she would tear the letter open, unable to wait, frantic for word. Instead, she lays it on the coffee table, then sheds her skirt and blouse, carefully hangs them up, and wraps herself in her (new) bronze bathrobe, winter-warm, but she's feeling a chill. Until finally here she is, curling herself into the wicker loveseat and picking up her letter.

The envelope is business-sized, impersonal as a bill. What does it smell like? Like an envelope, like mail. If there were ever traces of aftershave or prison, they have been lost in the boxes and bins and hands it has traveled through to reach her.

How brave Jane feels now, sliding her fingernail under the flap of the envelope.

There is a single sheet of paper inside. "Dear Jane Smith," it begins. The handwriting is smaller, but in the same style as that on the envelope, and the lines are closer together.

"Thank you for riting, I enjoyed recieving your letter, it was kind of you to take the time.

"My name is Brian Dexter. If you want to rite me again now you will be able to use my name exept on the envelope you will also have to use my number or I wont get your letter. Thats a rule here.

"As you can imagine there is a lot of rules here, probily for the good but sometimes its hard to know the sense of them. For example I can only rite two letters a month so I hope you dont mind that I couldnt rite you rite away and I mite not be able to anser every letter, should you decide to keep coresponding with me.

"I hope you will. It was nice to get your letter. Working in a libary must be nice, I was thinking maybe I could get a job in the libary here even tho I'm not much of a reader but it would be better than the kitchen which I do now.

"They keep us pretty busy and now it is 10 at nite and soon lites out so I will sign off for now. Like I said I hope you will rite again and I will too. It is nice to hear from a nice woman like yourself.

"Sinserly,

"Brian Dexter."

Oh dear. But what did she expect, eloquence?

Of course. Exactly. Eloquence, splendor, romance—all that (although she couldn't have said exactly what words she hoped for). This, though. Her heart feels squeezed.

She's just so very tired. For a few minutes she lets the letter lie in her lap; then sets out to read it again.

It reeks of sincerity, though, doesn't it, right down to the "sinserly" at the end? And after all, what if it had said, "I feel we are soul-mates, I will come to you on the wings of my release, my own true love" or some nonsense like that— how abrupt and terrifying! Far too much, too fast.

He thinks she's nice. Well, so she is.

And already he sees her as someone to emulate by getting work in the prison library (even if he thinks it's a "libary"). That's a start.

Who else does he write to? If he can write two letters a month, why can't they both be to her? Why should she have to wait? Why did she have to wait so long for this one?

Still, here it is.

There is some gentility, isn't there, in the phrasing of "should you decide to keep coresponding with me"? So he must have made some efforts to write his letter properly. It's too bad about the spelling and the grammar, but hardly hopeless. Perhaps he hasn't had Jane's opportunities. She could help.

He goes to bed early, too, just like her, although of course for him it's because of an arbitrary lights-out.

He enjoyed getting her letter. He says it was nice to get. He wants her to write again. He implies he will write her again. He, too, seems to assume a kind of future for them.

How much hope can one woman stand?

It will take some time to absorb what he's written. Obviously there is much more being said than just a single page of words.

She should have kept a copy of her own first letter. From now on she will; not only so she doesn't repeat herself, or contradict herself, but as a record: the progress of an unlikely but powerful romance. (And still she fails to ask important questions.)

She recalls offering to knit him a sweater, but he hasn't enclosed his measurements. Perhaps he doesn't realize that she'd be happy to, in return for the weeks of pleasure and anticipation and hope he's already given her.

Maybe next time. She can remind him.

Brian. A good name: solid and not a bit threatening, the name of an accountant, a life insurance salesman. Dexter, well, Dexter is slightly less sturdy, slightly closer to the edge of police blotters, perhaps. But then, to a Jane Smith, any more complex name is almost bound to have a somewhat shady sound.

Jane Dexter? Not bad. Jane and Brian Dexter. Brian and Jane Dexter. Together they sound like a suburban backsplit, with three bedrooms upstairs, kitchen and living room and dining room on the main floor, family room with fireplace downstairs, laundry, furnace and all those hidden things on the lowest level; the sounds of kids and animals outdoors, car doors slamming, street parties and communal barbecues.

Jane has been previously unaware of longings for street parties and communal barbecues.

Imagine, no sounds of odd parties floating up from the strange apartment underneath. (Nor would there be high ceilings or solid wooden banisters or only a short trip to her job, but these things are easily discardable, she suddenly finds.)

His letter is on unlined paper, and even so his handwriting is straight, going neither up nor down at the edges. That must say something about him: that he is a level-headed sort of man?

She spends the evening scrutinizing the letter for all the things it says about him. It's amazing how much there is, now that she's looking at it properly. One thing is how she could help him. She foresees knowledge and ambition as contributions she can make. And hope, which is what he has already given her.

The letter has one odd effect: she finds, when she goes to bed, early as usual, that there is something uncarnal, or even anti-carnal, about having this piece of paper on her bedside table; almost a witness. She wouldn't care to get carried away with it in the room.

What does she know about him that she didn't know this morning? His name. And that he works in the kitchen, and doesn't spell very well. That his real meanings must be camouflaged, his real words unwritten. That he is a watchful, precious sheet of white paper covered with handwriting Jane is already utterly familiar with, and terribly fond of.

She doesn't know (and doesn't wonder) who's more imprisoned: the man in his cell, writing his two letters a month (and doing heaven knows what else), or Jane in her bright little apartment, waiting and keeping her hands to herself. It seems there may be ways, whatever brutalities may occur to him (or be perpetrated by him, who knows?), in which his prison is more comforting and straightforward than Jane's.

Of course, for all we know (or Jane knows), he's one of those men who have already learned that. He may well be an astonishing recidivism statistic, as uneasy as Jane in the outside world, but with foolproof, if criminal, methods of escape back to the solid, welcoming, time-serving arms of jail.

As far as Jane's concerned, he is a wonderful, heartwarming, invisible mystery—hardly surprising that she falls asleep smiling. Because really, what a man.

5

"Dear Brian," she begins, and pauses. Should that be "Dear Brian Dexter," as he wrote to "Dear Jane Smith"? No, not if each letter is going to shift them closer to their radically informal future.

"Dear Brian, I was delighted to receive your letter, and pleased to learn that you were glad to get mine." Delighted, pleased, and glad, all in one sentence. She's going to sound like Mary Poppins!

"I'm surprised you're only allowed to write two letters a month. As you say, some rules seem awfully arbitrary, don't they?" Will he know what arbitrary means, or recognize it as a translation of what he wrote himself? Well, if he's thinking of working in the prison library, he'll have to learn to look up unknown words in the dictionary, that's Jane's view.

"I do hope, however, that you will decide to send one of those letters, which must be very precious, to me. I very much enjoyed your first one." She already said that, didn't she?

The point is, who would his second letter go to?

"You will think I am writing back very soon after your letter arrived here, but I expect to be quite busy in the near future, and may have less time." This is somewhat true: new and potentially exciting demands on her time are being made. "There is talk at my library of joining a union, which means lots of meetings and discussions. I don't know how it will turn out, but some people don't think they're being dealt with fairly. My friend Marcy said to me just today that I'm not, because I'm often asked to do other people's jobs as well as my own. Actually, I don't usually mind because I like being busy, but she's right in a way. What do you think of unions, Brian?"

What a thrill, using his name right in the middle of a letter, as if she can reach out and actually touch him, even from this distance!

"I think it's wonderful you might go to work in your library there. I'm sure it would be much more pleasant than the kitchen, and quieter, and you'd likely have more time to read yourself." But what if he isn't a man who likes quietness, or even pleasantness, and has no urge to read?

All she can do is nudge him in the right direction.

"I've been wishing I'd kept my first letter to you so that I could be sure I'm not repeating myself. Did I tell you I'm twenty-eight years old? I think I mentioned I have my own apartment, which I've recently been redecorating. I feel it's quite cozy, and look forward to coming home to it from work. It has comfortable furniture and light walls in different colors and some parts have wallpaper, although I think too much wallpaper can make even a big place feel too small, don't you?" Or is that cruel, reminding him sharply of his own confinement?

Written down, twenty-eight doesn't seem any great age. Unless of course he's much younger. She doesn't think he can be. She imagines he is in his thirties, possibly. So twenty-eight will seem just the right age to him.

"I also don't remember if I mentioned I'm a big sister. Do you know what that is? I act as a big sister to a little girl who doesn't have a father and whose mother is too poor or busy to take her all the places children should go. My little sister's name is Lydia, and she lives with her mother Lucy in a small apartment in a different part of town. I spend every Saturday afternoon with her, but have been thinking that I might give it up one of these days. Lydia is growing up, and I don't feel needs me so much any more."

That's a flat-out lie, and looks terrible written down like this. Still, it says a great deal: that Jane is a responsible woman with a variety of interests, including children; and that she has a generous heart, but at the same time is adaptable, and won't argue against abandoning vague obligations in favor of his attentions, when he comes bearing his attentions.

Anyway, under the circumstances, Lydia is disposable. No, too blunt a word. Expendable? Not that, either. Abandonable? All the words are mean ones. Can it be that all that's kept Jane from wickedness is circumstance and lack of opportunity? And that just a couple of small actions, like writing to Brian and buying new clothes, have turned her head? She finds the idea of being cruel appealing, now that she thinks about it: a woman accustomed to getting her own way, quite used to breaking hearts. So much power!

This must be how ends come to justify means. It's such a gentle, tempting slope, isn't it?

If he wonders about Lydia's circumstances and why she may need a big sister—well, Jane's not going to tackle that. Criminal acts are not subjects she wants to raise with him.

Other matters, however, do have to be faced. "I am trying to think of some other things you might like to know about me. One thing probably is, what do I look like. That's a hard thing to know about yourself, but I guess I could say I have brown hair and blue eyes, and I'm medium height. I'm not fat, but I'm not skinny either— just right, I like to think." Let him think that she is "just right" in every way. "I'm a quiet sort of person, but I also like a good time." Although considering it, Jane can't pinpoint just what would constitute a good time, besides, of course, the obvious.

"What else do you think you would like to know?"

No doubt he will describe himself, in his letter back to her. How can she trust what he says?

She rereads her description of herself and pictures him coming to her door. He may feel that she has lied, even though technically, perhaps, she has not. She is leaving an impression of a reasonably petite, still-young, blue-eyed brunette. Who will that make him think of? Some television star, perhaps, or some woman he knew back in the past Jane doesn't care to think about. "I wouldn't want you to think I was beautiful like somebody on television," she writes.

What if he asks for a picture? Or sends her one of him?

Actually, she really isn't prepared to see his face. The time for that will come, she imagines; longings will grow and change form until she is dying to know the shape of his cheekbones and his chin, the slant of his eyes, the tilt of his lips (not to mention the shape, slant, and tilt of the rest of him).

"I hope you will be able to answer this letter, even though you can only write two a month. I know I will be happy to respond." Oh, how happy she will be, this man has no idea! "Also I hope that even though we haven't met and don't really know each other, you will feel free to write anything you'd like. This is maybe a strange way to get to know somebody, but it's kind of nice, too, don't you think?"

She has in mind descriptions of his days, and what the place looks like and who the people are he knows and what sorts of things he thinks about when he's on his own. What he'd like to do or be. Who he is, if not who he's been—that's the kind of thing she'd like to know.

What if he feels free to write obscenities, or threats?

Impossible.

"Don't forget I could make you a sweater. If you send your measurements, I'd be happy to." She even bought beige wool today on her way home from an unexpectedly interesting day at work.

She will mail this in the morning. She hopes he writes back soon. She has just about sucked dry the possible meanings of the small misspelled words of his first letter.

Brian Dexter, confined too long, will not, she now realizes, be permanently content to stay upstairs here in her apartment, looking out her windows at the trees and sidewalks and the passing cars, waiting for her. He will, despite all his attentiveness—his lust, dare she say?— want to explore the larger world. Where will his taste in entertainments lie? In movies, nightclubs, or plays? Even operas or ballets? Or football, baseball, hockey games? Yes that, most likely. She can learn to enjoy those things, she's sure.

Her new hot pink, high-necked jacket, with enormous sleeves and a tucked-in buttoning at the hips, worn with black slacks, or white ones—that's a sporty sort of outfit, and appropriate, with the right top, even for bars. She would like to see the odd play, too (which does not seem possible to her, alone), and there are occasions like the library's Christmas staff party, until now an ordeal. How fine, how, oh, bursting and *male* he will be in his suit, a dark discreet blue, beside her in a simple plunging black dress, perhaps, that will also be bursting, hinting at great pleasureful secrets.

"Look at Jane!" people will say, nudging each other with not only astonishment but even envy. They will marvel at how complete and full she looks: coy, a demure and satiated animal. She foresees, especially if there's a union, all sorts of possibilities.

On her break, in the staff room today, she listened to Sheila and Marcy compare the quality of nailpolishes, and regarded her own hands. They were not what they might be, fingernails slightly ragged, knuckles dusty, the tendons on the backs of her hands as clear and ridged as if she were dying, flesh falling away. Or, sensitive and delicate, only the thinnest of thin skin layers protecting them from all the damage a dangerous world could be tempted to do to them. She considered her practical fingers. A man would hardly think of them moving through his hair, or touching him elsewhere, would he?

Jane blushed. Sitting in the staff room, right at the table with Sheila and Marcy, she made herself blush, imagining the elsewhere her fingers might travel.

She may go for a manicure one of these days.

When, eventually, he joins her, won't he wonder at the absence of friends? Won't he be puzzled that when her phone rings in the evenings, it's upholstery cleaning companies or people selling magazines?

To whose homes will they ever go to dinner?

What will her mother think of him?

"My mother and I," she can explain, "have never been close. We don't get along." That's not really a lie. And perhaps she can let him assume that her love for him has caused a dropping away of her friends.

Or perhaps if there's a union, she won't need to. It may open avenues its organizers haven't dreamed of.

Late this afternoon Marcy dropped by Jane's desk, perching on the corner, just when Jane was looking at the clock, gauging how soon she could leave. "You have a minute?"

"I guess so. Sure." Marcy'd never done this before, stopped for a chat. Not deliberately, anyway.

How do men sit in a bar and look at someone like Marcy and think, "I'm going to go over and introduce myself and ask her out, that's what I'm going to do"? How do they dare? How are they not terrified of feeling those big pale blue eyes scrutinize them and possibly find them wanting? Of hearing the soft, little-girl voice Jane imagines Marcy uses in places like that (although it's nothing like Marcy's work voice) say something like, "Are you kidding? Me, go out with you? Don't be silly."

Men really are brave.

Look at her prisoner. Jane would never have dreamed of advertising for companionship, but Brian Dexter, he thought about what he wanted and wrote down the words and paid money for the newspaper to run them and probably had no thought that he might be gambling with his pride.

Of course it was anonymously done. It wasn't as if his name, or his face, were actually attached to his words.

Still, the risk of getting no response! Or frivolous answers or cruel ones. Men are awfully exposed, aren't they, braving the possibility of being cut off, cut out, cut into?

"Listen, Jane. I don't know what you'll think of this, but even if you don't like it, please keep it a secret, okay?"

"Whatever," Jane said. "What is it?"

"Well, it's that a bunch of us have been talking about joining a union, and we were wondering, what would you think? Would you sign up with us?"

"A union? Why?" What an odd idea. And why would they care what Jane thinks?

"Because I guess we don't make very much money and we have to do jobs we weren't hired for and the pensions are terrible, stuff like that. Well, you know— you're all the time doing jobs you shouldn't have to, half the time you're out at the counter, or you're shelving books, and it's nice of you, but you're getting ripped off."

Has Marcy considered that one big reason Jane spends so much time on jobs not her own is that Marcy and the others don't do them properly?

There might be something to this.

"Will you at least come to a meeting, Jane? There's a union representative coming to my place tomorrow night, and we're all going to be there to talk about it and see what he has to say. Cheese and wine, just a relaxed thing. Will you come?"

By tomorrow night she'd be back to waiting. Already the prospect felt agonizing.

And maybe later, someday, she'd be able to invite Marcy and a couple of others to her place for an evening, so Brian would think that yes, these must be her friends. "I guess so. Sure, I could come, I think."

"You won't say anything to anybody though, will you, Jane? I mean, until we decide something, it really has to be a secret. People could get hurt."

Who did she think Jane could tell?

Well, she has mentioned it to Brian in her letter.

Maybe she *is* taken advantage of. Good old Jane will do it, may be what they say before sticking her with some job she wasn't hired to do at all. How pathetic, if she's good old Jane, that dutiful drayhorse, doing whatever she's asked.

"Can I bring something?"

"A bottle of wine if you like, but you don't need to."

Of course she does. Jane knows perfectly well you don't go to other people's houses empty-handed.

Is Brian a solidarity kind of man or a pull-yourself-up-by-your-own-bootstraps sort of individual? Are people who commit crimes generally more right-wing or left?

Perhaps their problem is anarchy.

When Marcy wrote down her address, Jane saw that it was only four blocks from her own place. Imagine, she and Marcy working together and living so close and never knowing!

When Brian comes, they might go out for a walk at night and run into Marcy, or other people from work visiting Marcy. She imagines them encountering each other, Jane and Brian walking arm-in-arm toward a bunch of them. "Why, there's Jane," they would say, and "What an amazing man she's with! Have you heard who he is? Do you know how they met? Isn't it just the loveliest story you've ever heard?"

Union has, of course, been much on Jane's mind, but of a different, warmer sort. This other kind, proposed by Marcy, could be both uncomfortable and dangerous. She could picture herself out on the sidewalk in winter, marching shyly up and down with a picket sign under the eyes of television cameras. Her nose would be red with cold, and she'd have to wipe it with her gloves. Her hair, dusted by snow, would be wet and wispy. What if a reporter asked her what she was doing and what her problems were?

Not at all how she has pictured herself on television.

But then, think of this: a picket line brawl. Irate library patrons or burly members of management trying to push their way through the lines, angry at being deprived of their books and videos and records. A hostile, mob-like atmosphere, vicious intentions clear. Elbows flashing out, a fist or two in evidence, maybe even a weapon. A brick or a baseball bat or a particularly heavy hardcover book. Jane and her picketing colleagues embattled and frightened, shrinking back.

But look, here comes Brian Dexter! He comes every day to walk Jane home, and just in the nick of time today. He pushes toward her, through the crowd, shoving people aside as if they were nothing, unarmed and weightless. He is more burly than any manager, pale and determined with anger. But calm.

People fall back, he parts the crowd like Moses entering the Red Sea, and the shouting and rude remarks are stilled. The television cameras follow him: to Jane, whom he embraces gently, wrapping his arms protectively around her shoulders, staring out at the mob with quiet menace. What would he say? The microphones would be close, the reporters approaching, but tentatively. Even the police would be stopped in their tracks, just watching.

Really, he would be doing them a favor: the force of his mere presence bringing peace.

Maybe he wouldn't say anything. Maybe he'd just stand there with her, facing them down until eyes dropped, feet shuffled and there was a quiet, embarrassed drifting away.

After a few minutes, other pickets would approach them. Marcy might touch him lightly on the sleeve.

"Thank you," she'd say. "We owe you. I don't know what might have happened."

He and Jane and everyone else would know that he acted for her. Oh, how lovely!

So yes, she could certainly welcome a union, especially if it actually led to something.

When Marcy left, with a quick grin and a quick hand on Jane's shoulder, Jane slipped into her new white and shiny raincoat, drawing the belt tight around her neat waist. On her tiny-heeled white shoes she clicked out of the office, turning off the fluorescent lights behind her, and strode briskly, eagerly, toward the front door.

What a striking man coming up the front steps to meet her, eyes and mouth smiling at the sight of her! Who could resist smiling back, how lovely, him coming here to walk home with her. A discreet hug, because they'd be in the library, after all, and then they'd turn, arms looped together, steps matching all the way home.

It was only tonight, writing the letter, that she thought to wonder about his view of unions.

Although in a way it doesn't matter. In her vision, he'd be looking out for *her,* not for worker solidarity.

And now, what an exciting tomorrow she has to look forward to: mailing her letter, which starts that cycle of delicious, fretful waiting again; and the meeting at night at Marcy's. A union—the idea is growing on her, implying whispered secrets, shared grievances—what drama! Already she feels stronger, and hardly alone. There is a lovely ripple of defiance, the nurturing of a sense of being hard done by, ripped off, taken advantage of by an enemy employer. A well-rounded life surely ought to have enemies as well as friends and lovers?

Jane's ambitions are increasing. Now they are: a lover, friends, and enemies. Major desires.

She can imagine herself becoming eloquent in the defense of workers, capable of stirring speech.

How reckless she is becoming, in her own pictures, in her own mind. The Jane who has a day like tomorrow ahead of her could turn into some radical woman!

Or not. She's just changing into her nightgown for an early retirement with the phantom prisoner when the phone rings, and it's not friend, enemy, lover, or even an upholstery cleaner or a magazine seller, but the thin high tones of her thin (and possibly high) mother.

"Jane?"

"Hi. What's wrong?" Jane can't imagine any reason for her mother to call, except for an emergency, and if her mother is calling, what sort of emergency can it be? She's the only family Jane has.

Jane sees her curled in the corner of her flowered sofa, a gin and tonic on a coaster beside the telephone and the pink frilly-shaded lamp on the end table. The light will be shining on her mother's hands and their immaculately red nails. Her mother's thin legs will be tucked up under her thin rear end, and her rope-veined arms will gesture as she speaks, although not so wildly that any of the gin and tonic will spill. She will likely be wearing her favorite pink housecoat, although it isn't very late, and her matching pink slippers will be on the floor. She won't, in short, look much like a mother at all.

"Nothing, I simply felt like calling you. See how you are."

"Well I'm fine. How about you?"

"Pretty good." What do other mothers and daughters talk about? "How's your job?"

"It's okay. We're joining a union." That's new, at least, and Jane finds it interesting.

"Really? I wouldn't have thought a library would be a likely place for a union." Jane wouldn't have, either, until today.

"People get ripped off there just like any place else, Mother." One of the things Jane finds irritating is the vagueness of her mother's impressions of her life. She seems to think working in a library is clean, a bit dull perhaps, but the very place for Jane. She has no idea what Jane actually does for a living. This is only one of her crimes of unmaternity, but it's a big one, in Jane's view.

"When do you think you might be coming for a visit, Jane?" What's that in her voice—some strain? An unfamiliar tone, anyway.

"I don't know, Christmas, I suppose. Why?"

"Are you especially busy these days?"

"Well, it's always busy." Oh, what a whirl of executive decisions and glamorous occasions Jane has to fit into her all-too-few hours, this fully occupied woman who is also, as it happens, talking on an end-table phone; and if it hadn't been for being interrupted as she changed, she'd also be wearing a housecoat. Her nails, unlike her mother's, may be neglected, but her skin is smooth and her veins show only in the very thinnest-skinned places. She is not like her mother at all.

Her mother has so many bad habits, not least of them the gestures she uses, tossing her hair and swinging her legs, even these days, when she's almost old.

It's a great thing, Jane thinks, that with Brian Dexter, she will be a whole new person. There will be no witnesses to the past.

"I know this is short notice, Jane, but since you can't come here, how would it be if I took a bus down to see you this weekend? Are you very busy then? We'd just have a little time together, you wouldn't need to change any plans."

What plans? Oh, cleaning the apartment, taking Lydia out, making up a new life—just the usual.

Her mother has never visited, and dislikes buses. "Sure, if you want to. Although I don't know how much time I'll have." Hours and hours: that's precisely the trouble. "But of course you're welcome. You could just make yourself at home." Oh God, what if she did? "But what's up? Why are you coming?"

"Do I have to have a reason? I thought it would be nice to see you. And your place. And I could do some shopping, get a few things I can't get here. So they'd be different from what other people have."

Shopping, that's why.

"But I don't want to stay long." As if Jane would ask her to. But why wouldn't she want to stay, does she foresee being too easily bored by her daughter? Or is there something that particularly requires her attention at home? A man, perhaps. That would also explain the shopping. Even the visit.

"Okay. Let me know when and I'll meet your bus." Where will her mother sleep? Not with Jane, in Jane's bed. If necessary, Jane will sleep on the loveseat and give her mother the bed.

Her mother may, come to think of it, be quite impressed by what Jane's done, all on her own, with this apartment. It would be nice to impress her.

But whatever will they talk about? And on a weekend, all the great holes in Jane's life will show up. It's out of the question to tell her mother what's really going on. There is no reason to suppose that her mother has grown gracefully into accepting what is real enough to Jane, if it seems to her mother to be a lie, any more than she has grown gracefully into her age, which is fifty-six.

"I'll take you out to lunch, Jane, if you find us a good place. Your choice, price no object." That little giggle, annoying, but familiar.

"Sure. But you know, I spend three hours every Saturday with my little sister Lydia. Maybe you can shop while I see her? It's not something I can get out of very well."

"Oh, but I'd like to meet her, why don't we all three go out together?"

Not Lydia *and* Jane's mother—might as well drag Lucy along as well. "If you want. I warn you, though, she's not exactly socially acceptable sometimes. A couple of hours with her can get pretty tiring." Because Jane's mother, whatever she thinks or feels, is no longer young, after all; and Jane gets just a little pleasure out of reminding her she's no longer that glamorous woman whose plain daughter was so difficult to appreciate.

"Oh, I'll manage," her mother says airily. Apparently she missed the point. "We'll have fun. So I'll see you then, okay?"

"Okay."

"Bye, honey."

"Bye."

It isn't until after she hangs up that Jane hears the "honey," and then she's amazed. Her mother, never one for endearments, might as well have said something really stunning, like "I love you."

Whatever her mother said, something peculiar is going on.

But of course—a man. Her mother must have plans; something romantic in the wind.

Jane has plans, too, but can hardly say to her mother, "Guess what? I've been writing letters to this guy in prison, Brian Dexter, and he writes me back. I have the most amazing ideas and pictures for when he gets out."

She has this dream. In it she is sitting on a straight-backed chair just inside the door of her apartment, with her hair done in an unfamiliar style, makeup on, scent dotted in the small dips of her neck where it meets her collarbones, and in the lines of her wrists and at the backs of her knees, and in the hollows underneath her ankle bones. She is wearing something long and pale, and her legs are crossed at the ankles, her knees are carefully together, her hands rest, holding each other, in her lap. She is the perfect picture of waiting.

In this scene, this dream, she sits patiently and still, listening keenly. She hears birds, she hears cars, she hears voices from the sidewalk and from the apartment below. She hears her own heart and her own blood. She hears rockets and guns being fired in countries an ocean away, and the cries of babies being nibbled at by rats or hunger. She hears the roars of men, enraged and violent, and the keening of women mourning their dead. She hears little girls skipping rope and laughing, and little boys rolling on dusty playgrounds. She can hear cries of ecstasy from bedrooms all across this city. She finds this not lonely, but an invitation.

Through it all, she is waiting for a particular sound: footsteps, men's boots on her stairs. They move slowly, one step at a time, not quite heavy and certainly not menacing, but firm and sure. The door would open and there he'd be: a grand orchestra of a man containing all those other sounds himself.

This picture leaves Jane almost unbearably optimistic. She can almost feel her heartbeats and the currents of her blood. It's such a pleasant vision, so agreeably dramatic. What a pity it has to be a secret.

What would her mother say? Well, probably nothing very different from what any mother would say. Something like, "Are you crazy? You know nothing about this man, you don't know why he's in prison, or if he's ever getting out, or if he even wants to meet you, or if that would be safe. What gets into you, Jane? You are the oddest child."

Even though, of course, Jane is no child. She is twenty-eight, and pretty soon she's going to be twenty-nine. That only leaves thirty. Events must occur.

And so they will. Just, they're nowhere near ready for exposure to outside light or air, and certainly not to her mother's brisk, harsh breath.

Jane doesn't know much about this man, that's true. She doesn't know why he's in prison, or if he's ever getting out, or if he really wants to meet her, or if that would be safe. But she isn't crazy. She is absolutely positive that even if it's fragile now, in the end all this makes perfect sense.

6

Jane, marching briskly off to work this morning, pauses at the corner mailbox just long enough to drop in her second letter. This time there's not a twinge that there might be regrettable consequences.

She walks all the way to the library, unwilling to sit still on a bus.

Her fingers fly over the keys of her word processor, cranking out letters, printing out memos.

The faster she works, the more rapidly time will pass, speeding events. She sets a pace that should be infectious: spreading beyond the library doors, to the street, to the mailbox, to the post office, where her letter will be handled swiftly but also conscientiously by workers caught by her efficiency. There will be no traffic jams or detours for trucks heading out on highways, no mailbags sent inadvertently in the wrong direction. More: there will be no line-ups at the liquor store when she stops by later to buy wine. And as the effects spread right across the city and into its corners, Lydia will pay acute, inspired attention in her classroom, and Lucy may take a stab at cleaning their apartment. Jane feels as if all this day's righteous moments will flow out of her flying fingers.

Certainly time does fly for her.

What's Brian doing now? He's in the prison kitchen, likely, preparing lunch for hundreds. That must take hours every morning, and then more hours every afternoon, preparing dinner. Jane makes her own lunch in a matter of moments each day before she leaves for work: today a salmon sandwich and a small bagged bunch of seedless grapes. Sometimes she eats in her tiny office, but more often in the staff room, where there's always coffee brewing and the sound, at least, of voices, even if they're not addressing her. There's such a thing as too much silence.

Brian's world must be filled with sound: the constant rumbling of men's deep voices.

What is his voice like? How will he say her name?

Jane can work very hard and quickly without thinking much about it. It's quite mechanical, what she does, typing and addressing, filing and keeping things in order. Without Jane and her precise sort of care, with just an ordinary worker, things at this library might very well fall apart, she thinks.

Does anybody else know that? That she is indispensable?

Perhaps a union will make it clear. There is that meeting tonight, something to look forward to, and be wary of.

People seem to think nothing of stopping by her doorway, even though she's clearly occupied. Here's Mrs. Curtis, tall and efficient (although no more efficient than Jane), her long dark hair pulled back in a librarian's bun, although it looks glamorous on her, not frumpy like a librarian cartoon. Her bones are angular, that's why. They make her look like someone in charge. Perhaps that's why she's in charge: she simply looks as though she ought to be.

If Jane's so good at her job, why hasn't she been pro-moted? Mrs. Curtis hired her. She ought to recognize Jane's value.

Maybe people who are good at what they do and cause no problems simply don't get noticed. That's not fair. Jane looks at her, aggrieved.

"Jane," Mrs. Curtis says, "would you mind taking a few minutes at the shelves? We're getting behind out there again. If you could spare a half hour or so, it'd be a real help."

No doubt. And who is ever asked to help Jane? Not that it would ever be necessary. Not that she would ever want help. Someone else would only get in her way.

It's the principle, though. Fairness. The point of a union.

Which of course is a secret.

Jane hears herself saying, in a chilly, unfamiliar voice, "But that's not my job, you know. That wasn't in the description of my work when I was hired."

Oh my. Mrs. Curtis's eyebrows rise and her mouth drops open, so that there's an amazed sort of space in between. Jane hears her own words, in that peculiar voice, hanging in the air, and can't believe what she's done. Was that her?

"Can it wait till I finish this?" gesturing at the small heap of papers on her desk. "Then I can get right to it." Now she sounds timorous. Why can't she get her voice right?

"Certainly. Whenever you can." Mrs. Curtis stands in the doorway for a moment longer, regarding Jane, and Jane knows but keeps her head down. What a narrow escape!

Think what might have happened! She might have been shouted at, or even fired on the spot. Well, perhaps not fired. It may cost her a raise, though, or part of one. What did Mrs. Curtis see, some loud-mouthed rabble-rouser? At any rate, not the usual Jane at all.

The moment abruptly changes her outlook on the day, so that she is no longer on a roll of good fortune.

Jane does her job, she earns her pay, and anyway, who wants a union? It must be Marcy, or someone like her, who isn't working hard enough, as usual, or Jane wouldn't be called on to help.

What possessed her, to speak in that tone of voice? Did she consider herself, just for a little while, charmed?

Now what if she buys the wrong wine, or makes a fool of herself at the meeting at Marcy's tonight? Or gets mugged going home in the dark, like poor Mr. Alexander?

Worse, worst: what if her letter is lost, or says all the wrong things, or remains in competition with letters from other smarter, prettier, more interesting, more scented women?

How suddenly Jane can foresee disaster, dooming herself.

"You're still coming tonight, right?" Marcy whispers, as they work (or Jane works, Marcy lingers) at the shelves: around the Vs, at the far end of the great room of books, where they're unheard and unseen.

"I guess so." She'd rather not, now. But she has mentioned it to Brian, and he'll want to know how events are progressing, won't he?

Maybe. Depending on his other letters. Depending on his degree of interest.

Anyway, simply for her letters to have some plot, some movement of character and event, conflict even, she is going to have to get out more. Just as her mother used to recommend.

Oh dear, her mother is coming this weekend. How did she manage to forget that?

Best to keep busy. Although that will make the weekend seem to come faster. Isn't it something, though, that time no longer stretches out ahead of her in its old waiting-to-be-filled way?

In the liquor store on the way home, she is relatively bold, asking for help to find something good. Home, she gets out the beige wool, just for an hour or so, before the meeting. She may not have his measurements, but she has her visions and can at least make a start, casting on.

Should she take her knitting with her? It would give her something to do with her hands. What would she say, though, if they asked, and surely they would, what she was making and who it was for?

Marcy's street is familiar. It's in Jane's neighborhood, and she must have walked along it before for one reason or another, but tonight it has new aspects. Because this is Marcy's street: because someone she knows, however poorly, walks here too, looks into these windows, maybe says hello to some of the people in these houses, if they're outside, or even visits them inside, is friends with them. Marcy's life, if it's anything at all like Jane's (but of course it's not), is focused on her home, this block, the sounds of these cars, those birds, the boys in that yard tossing a football back and forth.

It seems a pleasant, ordinary, family kind of street, with more of those big sturdy maples. Most of the houses are for single families, but there is the odd one, as on Jane's block, broken into two or three apartments. Marcy's place turns out to be one of those. Like Jane's, the building is old and brick and elegant, if fading, but Marcy's apartment, unlike Jane's, is on the ground floor.

There is a tricycle tipped over in the entranceway. How inconvenient to live where there are children upstairs—the noise, and this sort of thoughtless untidiness, toys left about in the way of adults. This sort of thing reminds Jane how fortunate, really, she is herself. As long as the men downstairs live there, her home is wonderfully peaceful.

She was afraid of being late, but appears to be early. She foresees an evening spent watching and listening, trying to think of something to say. She will be able, though, to anticipate going home, where she has love waiting for her (although love will have to vacate temporarily, when her mother comes).

Maybe the wine she's brought is wrong? The man at the liquor store called it "medium-priced" but "adequate." It cost fifteen dollars, though, and to the others, that may well be too much. She hopes it doesn't make her look too eager to please or ostentatious. It's these small things that count, either for or against a person.

Marcy has a doorknocker in the shape of a horse's head. Does Marcy like horses? Maybe she's a country girl, Jane wouldn't know, although Marcy always seems very urban to her. Jane doesn't know the first thing about her, really, and discovers precisely that soon after Marcy opens the door.

"Jane, how nice." Marcy smiles. "I'm so glad you've come."

"I brought this," stiffly holding out the wine.

"That's great. Oh, it really *is* great," drawing it out of its bag, holding it up. "I've got some cheap stuff, but we'll have yours first so people can appreciate it." Obviously it is too expensive, but Marcy has made that into a treat and a virtue. That's kind of her; maybe she's not so silly.

"You're the first one here." But didn't she hear Marcy talking to somebody as she approached the door to let Jane in? "Come on into the living room and we'll get a head start on the others."

Marcy's apartment, Jane notes, could use some fresh paint. Her furniture is clearly old and secondhand, the sofa a dark green, the two soft chairs gray, the coffee and end tables a cheap dark veneer. Everything looks worn. Is she really paid so poorly? Maybe she spends all her money entertaining herself. No wonder she wants a union, and more money.

Wouldn't she hesitate to bring men back here? It's not exactly a seductive atmosphere. Even the light is too bright.

There's a red and black blanket in a heap on the floor. If Jane had been having this meeting at her home, the place would have been spotless, the lighting discreet, the atmosphere enticing. Even for co-workers, she would have made quite an effort. Perhaps if there is another meeting, she could host it. People might be surprised.

"Babes," Marcy calls, startling Jane, "come and meet one of my friends from the library."

Babes? A man here? She calls Jane one of her friends— well, that's nice.

This is Marcy's surprise: a little blonde person, fine hair pulled into a ponytail, appears in the doorway, dressed in a white cotton nightgown dotted with pink and blue flowers. "Jane, I'd like you to meet my daughter, Simone. Simone, this is Jane Smith."

This is impossible. Marcy, a mother? Marcy, who seems just a child herself, whose conversations (as far as Jane has been aware) lean toward dates and nailpolish and diets, comes home every evening to this small lovely person? Has Simone been a secret, or has Jane not been listening? She's never heard her mentioned, she is sure.

"Hello, Simone, it's very nice to meet you." Jane knows she has spoken in that too-loud voice unaccustomed adults use with children, as if children are deaf or stupid. But she wasn't ready for this.

"Hello." Simone sounds shy, and is looking at the floor.

"I didn't know you had a child," Jane ventures.

"Really? Oh yes, Simone's almost four now, aren't you, Babes? I guess I don't talk about her much at work. I mean, I can't stand it when other people go on and on about their kids, like why should anybody care, so I try not to. Anyway," and Marcy hugs her child and laughs, "Simone's too special to talk about, aren't you, Babes?"

Jane knows just what Marcy means: she understands about matters too important to chat about.

It's funny, but Marcy looks different here, not the way she looks at work, although she has her makeup on and her hair is as smooth as ever and her fingernails are shining a rosy pink. It's her expression, soft somehow, and her casual jeans and T-shirt, Jane decides, that make a difference.

"I guess I didn't even know you were married."

What a blunder, she realizes as soon as the words are out. Everyone knows a child is no proof of marriage.

"I was. Not any more."

"But you're so young."

"Oh, I'm afraid I'm not, you know." Marcy smiles. "But thank you. I'm twenty-seven." Jane would have thought twenty-one, twenty-two, a mere infant.

A year younger than Jane, and Marcy has gone through a marriage and is raising a child, apparently all by herself;

while all this time Jane has just been waiting. She could by now have had a four-year-old child herself. Or a ten-year-old one, for that matter. "Simone's an unusual name. Is your family French?"

"No." Marcy laughs. "My husband and I were watching an old Simone Signoret movie when I went into labor, and it seemed right at the time. Actually it still seems right, even though it's a bit fancy, I guess. Anyway, I just call her Babes, don't I, Babes?"

Simone lifts her head, smiles at her mother, and Jane, watching, sees a lost world. Imagine being regarded like that!

Perhaps she has misjudged the allure of children. Or their capabilities. There doesn't seem to be anything very frightening about Simone, no glances at Jane implying she sees things her mother doesn't, in that keen, un-guarded view of childhood.

Of course Simone would not be so appealing if she was loud or crying or mischievous, instead of sweetly behaved and shy. It hardly seems fair that a woman Jane knows for her carelessness should have this child. Like Jane's mother, Marcy seems to have more than her share.

When the others start arriving, Marcy tells Simone to get ready for bed. Jane wants to ask that she be allowed to stay up. When Simone asks to have a story read to her, Jane wants to volunteer, but Marcy hands Simone a pic-ture book, and the little girl obediently vanishes. Jane misses her. She seems to have altered the texture of the room and of Jane's part in this gathering.

People are talking now about danger: how they could be punished if managers found out their plans. Ordinarily this would likely be Jane's concern as well, since she is not precisely brave, nor exactly sympathetic to the grievances of people who don't do their jobs right in the first place. If she were very brave, she might just say: "Why don't you do your work before you start talking about how badly you're treated?" That would, of course, be very unwise; anyway, these are larger matters than she has considered before. Maybe if Marcy doesn't concentrate on shelving books with absolute accuracy, it's because other concerns occupy her. Maybe she has to worry about who's taking care of Simone, or how the child is feeling or how she's going to afford a Christmas or a birthday gift? Obviously Marcy has far more on her mind than Jane would have dreamed. The others may, too. It could be only Jane whose thoughts are at liberty to concentrate on the alphabet.

She and Marcy can't be the only ones in this room who have secrets. This makes her, in a way, one of them, and somewhat sympathetic, so she signs the union card. It seems the least she can do for these people, with their mysterious and unexpectedly complicated lives.

"I'm glad, Jane," Marcy says. "I wasn't sure how you'd feel about it. I guess we were a little nervous asking you, so this has been a nice surprise. Except you haven't said much."

Jane shrugs. "There's nothing to say, really. I think it's a good idea."

"And you're not nervous about it?"

Again she shrugs. "Why should I be? I do my job." (Will any of them catch the hint?) "What can they do to me?" As if she really were a brave woman. How fine to have these people admiring her sturdy courage. It makes her feel like a different woman: someone with spark and vigor and even qualities of leadership. Why, perhaps she could even run for the executive, when the time comes. These people seem to see something in her. The perception could so easily become reality. This is Jane's experience; so maybe the trick is just to have different perceptions?

There are only eight, no nine, people here. Not one of them holds an important position, or at least one with an important title. What makes them think they can change anything? What makes them think that even together, they have any power?

One of the security guards (more interesting-looking out of his uniform, in jeans and red sweatshirt—but too old, in his fifties, maybe, anyway much older than Brian must be) pours Jane another glass of wine. "It's good," he says, "having somebody like you here." Someone like her?

"Why?"

"Because you get respect. They like what you do. Here too, the people here," waving his hand around the room. "Everybody knows you work good. I like that you always say hello to a person, too. Some don't."

Respect. There's a word Jane hasn't considered. Imagine, people have talked about her! They have spoken of her in flattering terms. They have each of them, perhaps, thought of her, admired her, in the privacy of their own homes.

She has rarely spared any of them a thought, except to picture their good times together. She speaks to this security guard every morning, passing his desk, because it's hardly possible to ignore somebody sitting right there. She hasn't considered it a kindness.

Everyone seems open to misinterpretation. It appears that this can be to her benefit.

She might grow into this part. She might become unbearably respected, intolerably kind. There are glimpses here of entirely new and different Janes, far more alert ones.

"Thank you," she says to him. Politely. And "Thank you," she says to Marcy at the door, as she leaves. "I'm glad you asked me." Even to say so much leaves her vulnerable: what if Marcy isn't glad at all?

But why wouldn't she be? Jane is respected.

Walking home, she continues to believe in her own courage and capacity, for most of the way. Is this how other people feel in their ordinary moments?

Now, unlocking her apartment door, she sees not only Brian but a small child waiting for her. Dark-haired, but otherwise much like Simone, with china skin and chubby legs and blue eyes lighting up. She would be beautiful.

Or she might be plain. If she were plain, Jane would love her even more, knowing how necessary that is.

The child would run to her, and they'd hug each other. She would tell Jane all about her evening. She wouldn't be anything like Lydia; nor would Jane resemble Lucy. There'd be just the two of them.

No, there wouldn't. There'd be Brian, too. A child needs a father, and a child would be good for him, settle him down, give him a sense of responsibility and love. Jane and a child would be his rehabilitation. How warm, coming home to them both.

How crowded! There is certainly not room here for three people. She'd have to move.

Oh, she would miss this place! She has had so many tender moments here, with hands and letters and plans. How could she start again somewhere else? All that painting and wallpapering and careful choosing of just the right furniture, all over again in a bigger place—a tiring thought.

But in a suburban split-level, a transformable beige, her whole life could become blessedly ordinary.

People move on. There are always great fresh fields of opportunity, of pleasure and excitement.

How terrifying. And interesting.

In her bedroom, changing into her nightgown, she takes a moment to lean over a small phantom bed, to check on a small phantom child. How rosy she would be, how damp-curled and innocent, lying there. What stupendous love! Jane can feel stupendous love right now, so imagine how great it would be if there were a real child lying here.

Because she knows there isn't. Any more than Brian is in the living room, watching television and waiting for her to emerge in her nightgown, to curl up on the loveseat with him for a while before they head off to bed. Jane does know that.

She wonders how Marcy manages. Does she get money from Simone's father? Apparently she hasn't much money—although, Jane reminds herself, she does have enough to go out to bars, meeting men and having dates. If Jane were Marcy and had a child waiting at home, she doesn't see how she'd be able to do that. Maybe Marcy isn't as fine a mother as she seemed tonight. Anyway, Jane would be a far, far better one.

Marcy must have had to organize child care during the day, and that can be expensive, as well as worrying. Would Jane keep working? What would it be like, being home all day with a child?

Anyway, she'd have Brian. He would help. She's sure he'd be so entranced by fatherhood he'd *want* to help.

Then the child would love him hugely, too, and something about that feels a little disconcerting.

Her letter will be on its way to him tonight. Even as she lies here reading herself to sleep, it is passing through machinery and hands and trucks, moving toward him.

Does he sleep on his side, like her, or on his back (which could mean he snores), or on his stomach? Does he lie peacefully through the night, or thrash about in his dreams? What kinds of dreams does Brian Dexter have? Does he look sweet, or closed up and remote?

She watches the sleeping head on the pillow next to hers, tracing lines and angles with her eyes: how beautiful. She would stay awake all night, to watch such a sight as a sleeping man. Still this person doesn't have a face.

Would he want to rest with his arms around her, holding her the way heroes do? Or would he be a solitary sleeper, keeping to his own side, at most holding her hand? She wouldn't mind that, if she knew that anytime she woke up, she could watch him.

They could go to sleep curled together like the spoons her books describe: so warm and reassuring to have a body folded around hers, an arm folded across her. His chin would rest on the top of her head, her head would nestle into his chest. In that position, who could hurt her?

If there were an intruder (not impossible) he would know what to do. He would leap up and defend her and her possessions. She could sleep soundly, knowing that.

It'll be interesting at work to see what happens, now that this rebellion has begun. There may be secretive glances, raised eyebrows, small discreet hand signals among the staff, like spies identifying one another, and Jane will be among those who understand.

People may want to go for a drink after work to discuss events, and Jane would be included, naturally. Oh, she is part of a great movement: toward equity and fairness, power to the people who do the real work.

Or, as in the case of Marcy and a few of the others, who don't do the real work.

Never mind. Marcy has her reasons, she has her problems. And she called Jane her friend. That was nice.

Maybe she should, after all, start taking Lydia to the museum, the art gallery, take out a library membership for the child. Even if Lydia doesn't want to do any of those things, Jane could show some leadership. "Just try it," she could urge. "Keep at it. I promise you, you'll be glad in the end." Jane would learn some things, too. She would have far more to talk about if she knew something about sculptures and paintings or old artifacts. Or books, for that matter, besides her romances, which are a vice, something kept secret the way some people drink.

Then, once Lydia was presentable and Jane had some interesting expertise, perhaps she could invite Simone and Marcy to come along with them some Saturday. They could go to a good restaurant and have a decent meal. She's sure Simone would know how to behave, and by then Lydia would, too. The girls would be friends, despite the difference in age, not to mention experience. They would chatter with each other while Jane and Marcy—while Jane and Marcy what? They could talk about union plans, maybe. Or child care, who knows? "This is really nice of you, being a big sister, Jane," Marcy might say. "I never knew."

"Well," Jane would answer, "I guess it just never came up."

Marcy might smile. Laugh out loud, even. "You do hide your light under a bushel, don't you?"

A pleasing way to look at it.

Of course, so much depends on Brian. He will have demands of his own on her time.

Jane has no idea why she has this firm notion he'll be getting out of prison, but she's as sure of it as she is of anything, everything, else.

How very large and populated and busy her world is becoming, who knows where it might end? A family of ten in the suburbs, and Jane as president of the local PTA, or running for the school board. A gracious hostess, with a handsome husband of exotic, slightly dangerous and mysterious background. Plain, to be sure, but doesn't she have something, that spark that makes it easy to overlook her features? Then she would be "just Jane," comfortable and admirable, and quite a different matter from "plain Jane."

This, now, is just the start, this new view of herself.

Respected. That's fine.

Maybe by this weekend, while her mother visits, he'll be handed her letter. And even be writing back. In prison, are weekends a kind of slack, open time, the way they are on the outside?

Or maybe, unable to wait, he's already written her again. Maybe his letter is on its way now, crossing hers in the mail, carrying word of prison life, and his desires.

For all she knows, Brian Dexter is lying on his bunk right now imagining a life with that nice young Jane Smith he encountered so serendipitously through his advertisement, in her tasteful pastel-and-wicker apartment, with her books, her intelligence, her good job with its steady income, her kindness, her beautiful (he may be sure) body.

And her imagination, of course. Let's hope, if any of this is the case, that he is also imagining her imagination. He should see it as darting farther and farther afield, landing here and there and taking off again. Who knows where it might wind up?

Not Brian Dexter; not Jane, for that matter. Jane doesn't see an end in sight, and wouldn't care to.

7

This gift of Jane's for story-making is by no means recent. Her way of devising visions that are just as real as real is as old as her memory. Now, she may be endowing an unknown man with certain properties, inclinations, and intentions; adult pictures. But even as a child, the pictures weren't exactly innocent. Even then they had to do with justice, or at least fairness, a balancing of out-of-kilter scales.

How would a child have known that? Well, she wouldn't have, really; would just have been groping toward comfort or sense.

People, then, were hardly involved, but what a flair for plot she had! Involving, in those days, mainly animals: squirrels and raccoons and even bears. Brian has his bear-like aspects, too.

There was a huge pine tree in the back yard of their home, dark blue-green and looming. Jane sat under it, a little figure, hands clasped around knees, eyes closed, listening. Squirrels raced along branches, telling tales, such gossips. She liked this world.

"Listen," they chattered, talking fast so she had to pay very close attention, "do you know about the bears? In

101

that bush on the road out of town? There are bears, but they're all right, they're pretty friendly, and anyway they only come into town at night." So those must be the sounds she heard, waking in her room in darkness, rustlings in the yard below. "Don't worry, they like kids all right. What they do is, they look in people's windows and see who's doing bad things and good things." And then at some unspecified future time they made judgments, plotting punishments and rewards. This was how it came about that people Jane heard her mother discussing on the phone, or in the kitchen with friends, came to suffer disappointment, endure tragedy, enjoy some particular good fortune. Because of the bears. It made perfect and comforting sense, knowing *somebody* was in charge of fairness, good that it was someone large and calm and powerful, removed from situations, capable of unflawed dispassion.

No matter what happened, Jane could rely on the judgments of the bears.

Raccoons, more impulsive and sweet-natured, hid gifts in garbage cans, where clever, good humans would find them, if they looked. So Jane, convinced, regularly went through the family trash in search of treasure. Because she was good, wasn't she? Perhaps not good enough. She was always disappointed, but always hopeful.

There was terrible news one day, though: something awful in that bush, waiting and watching for a particular moment of weakness, keen eyes on Jane, so helpless and small a target. The squirrels went on and on about it, skittering and leaping through the pine branches as Jane huddled below.

She was so upset she even told her mother. A mistake, but it shouldn't have been, should it? Shouldn't a mother have comforted and promised to protect? Jane was only, what, four? Before she started school, anyway. This is one of the first things she can remember with any clarity.

"Mummy!" She was tugging at her mother's dress, they were in her parents' bedroom, her mother was stripping the bed for the wash. "I got a sister, did you know that? Mummy?" She had to keep pulling at that dress, try to get her mother to slow down, pay attention, *help* her.

"What? For heaven's sake, Jane, stop yanking on my clothes."

"But Mummy, she lives in the woods and she looks just like me so nobody can really tell she isn't me, except she's really bad, she steals and lies and sometimes she hurts the animals, they told me. Her name's Anna, did you know?"

And here was the worst part, and her mother wasn't stopping, she'd gathered the bedding and was headed out of the room. "Mummy!" Jane on her little legs hurrying after. "She wants to *steal* me. So she can live here instead and you won't know because she looks just like me. She's going to *do* that, and you won't even know and I'll have to live in the bush and you'll never *see* me again." By now she was weeping with terror, frantic and clutching at her mother's legs. Oh help, help, she was pleading, she can remember that, although the words didn't get said out loud. But what kind of mother wouldn't hear them anyway?

This was the truest story she knew, right at that moment. That she would disappear and nobody would notice. "How bad Jane's become," people would say. "What's come over her? She used to be so good and quiet." They'd never dream it wasn't Jane at all, but that mean and mischievous twin. Malevolent, if Jane had known the word then.

"Jane." Her mother stopped, turned, looked down but went on holding her armful of sheets. "Stop this right now. I'm busy and you're being silly."

"But Mummy, it's true!"

"It isn't true at all." Why wasn't that reassuring? Why didn't Jane believe her for an instant? "Go on now, go outside and find somebody to play with and stop making things up. You mustn't tell such lies."

To be not only plain but a liar: cruel judgments, surely, from a mother.

It was the end of sitting under that tree listening to the squirrels. She didn't want to hear any more. Perhaps disbelief was what she deserved. She had broken a confidence, had spoken out loud, to someone outside the magic, words she should have kept to herself.

For a long time she remained frightened of that abrupt vanishing, though: that moment when she wasn't quite alert and could be snatched into some place that was no place. It took a while for that to go away. She would never again tell her mother a secret, no matter how frightening. That didn't go away.

From now on she would keep her pictures and plots to herself. So they couldn't be touched.

Funny, that she hasn't forgotten. And that remembering, she still has a sense of reality about that twin: that she's still out there. Perhaps not so wicked or malevolent; maybe just more interesting. Maybe they could talk like sisters. Anna. Where did that name come from?

But that interesting girl, woman now, might steal Brian, as she might once have stolen Jane.

A little kid, tearing around the bus depot, bumps into Jane, jolting her arm, making her coffee splash. Where has she been? Evil twins, for goodness sake! She shakes her head to clear it, and the child darts away as if avoiding a blow.

Her mother's bus is late and Jane, of course, was early getting here this morning. What a dreary place! Oh, it's been tarted up on the outside, and inside there are brightly painted walls and vivid plastic benches instead of the old dark wooden ones, efforts have been made, but apparently no one has been able to tart up the people, hunched in their seats, drinking coffee from throwaway cups, waiting apathetically to be moved from this place to some other place. Not like airports, where there's a sense of will and purpose, people deciding and acting to take themselves elsewhere.

Or so it seems to Jane.

That little kid—well, there are actually two of them, probably brother and sister, and none too clean, the boy maybe six, the girl about four, both of them racketing around. Where is their mother, why isn't she keeping better control over them? Or, Jane supposes, where is their father?

Jane's little girl would be clean, well dressed, and well behaved. Jane wishes she were here now.

What sort of grandmother would Jane's mother be? Doting? Hard to imagine. If Jane had a daughter, would Jane's mother be stepping off a bus now with her arms loaded with gifts, toys, and clothes? Baked goodies from home? Would she inadvertently rake Jane's daughter with her long red fingernails and recommend ways in which her hair might be improved? Would she say to Jane something like, "What a shame, dear, she doesn't seem to know what to do with herself, does she? But then, you never did, either, did you?"

Even Jane admits that her mother is never so bluntly cruel.

And here is the bus now. And here comes Jane's mother, finally, waving gaily. The two of them, she in a brilliant red rain coat, Jane in her shiny white one, will look something like a pair of tulips bouncing together through the city today.

They embrace lightly. Jane exposes her cheek to be touched briefly by her mother's lipsticked lips. Her mother steps back, hands on Jane's shoulders. "My dear, you look wonderful, altogether different. So bright!"

And so, with her mother's first words, it begins: that Jane has undergone new and radiant improvements; but that for twenty-eight years she has lacked wonder and brightness. She needs to take a deep breath. "You too. I like your coat."

"Thanks. It was a treat for myself. I felt like something bright. We're a pair, aren't we?" Jane, who has never thought of them as a pair, finds the idea difficult.

The two rowdy youngsters have been claimed by a tidy young woman. She looks respectable and quiet with her brown hair, brown coat, brown shoes, as she herds the children toward a bus, a hand on each head. It's a pleasant-looking scene. Perhaps, Jane thinks, some parents don't realize that not everyone shares their enthusiasm for their children. She must remember, herself, when the time comes, that her miracle will not necessarily be everyone's.

"Is this all your luggage?" One bag, stuffed and heavy, but small.

"All I need, just for overnight. You know, the trip wasn't nearly as bad as I expected. I can't think why I haven't done it before." Oh dear, what if she makes a habit of it? What would Brian say, her mother calling every few weeks to announce her arrival for a couple of days? "Only to pick up a few things," she might say. "Your stores are so much better than anything here."

"I'm sorry it's raining." As if it were Jane's fault. "What sort of things did you want to look for?"

"What?" Her mother looks confused for a moment. "Oh, you mean shopping. Well shoes, I suppose, maybe a couple of dresses. Nothing too strenuous." Enough to account for this impetuous visit?

"Then let's drop your stuff at my place first. Come on, the cab stand's out this door." Jane herself might walk, except for the rain, since it's not terribly far. "I'll show you where I work. We go right past the library on the way."

Even now, Jane can still be caught, impressed, by the view of the library: broad sturdy stone building, with its great wooden double doors and rows of narrow old windows. It can still seem to her like a magic place, containing shelf after shelf of the unknown, secrets, knowledge. She thought, to begin with, that this was a place where much would come clear.

Her mother, though, seems only mildly interested. "Mmmm, quite grand, isn't it?"

Her mother doesn't know a blessed thing about Jane's life.

"I told you we're forming a union, didn't I?"

"Union?" The cabbie leans his head back. "Bunch of lazy, spoiled people, figure the world owes them a living."

If Jane were another sort of person, she would speak up. She might do what her mother does, which is raise her eyebrows, freeze her voice, and say, rather slowly, "I don't believe that when we hired you, we were also asking your opinions?"

The driver's head snaps forward. "Fuck you, lady," he says, not quite under his breath. Jane hopes her mother didn't hear. She wonders if her mother would be shocked. Perhaps her mother isn't shocked by many words, or by much of anything at all.

Anyway, she wishes she were as quick and fierce as her mother. Of course, one reason it's hard to be close to her mother is that very sharp tongue. It can be, as the cabbie just learned, a perilous business coming within reach of it.

"But Jane, this is delightful," her mother exclaims as she steps through Jane's door. "You have wonderful taste. I could never have imagined your place would be like this." See? Those two painful and conflicting messages again.

"Thank you. I'll show you the bedroom. You can hang up your things. Do you want to lie down for a while?"

"Heavens no, why on earth would I? It's not even noon yet. Do we have far to go?"

"No, the good stores are pretty close. Everything's close here."

"That's strange. To me, it seems awfully big." Well it would, wouldn't it, coming from a small town? Jane feels cheerfully cosmopolitan.

What does her mother's social life consist of, after all? A few card games and visits with friends. Outings, Jane has to accept, with men. Or a man. Bars, a movie now and then, evenings of television. Hardly stimulating. If somewhat livelier than Jane's.

"I do like this house," her mother says, running her hand along the banister as they head back downstairs.

"Me too." It's nice, to look at it from another person's point of view. Reassuring. Brian, too, will be impressed.

Another taxi, driven by a silent man, takes them downtown. "I have these terribly *small* feet, you see," Jane's mother tells the shoe store clerk. "It's so difficult to get fitted properly. I do hope you can help me." The way she looks at him—at her age!—seems to make him want to help her. How does she do that?

Why does he notice?

Could Jane?

When Brian comes, will she find that sort of thing coming naturally to her: the looking up at him from under demure eyelids, the way of standing, slanted slightly sideways, in a supplicating sort of way? Will her hands go out toward him, palms up that way, asking for something?

Jane thinks she'd likely just look foolish. Watching her mother, she thinks she looks foolish, too. Because she's old; or not young. There's some age after which these methods are unseemly.

Her mother is brisker dealing with the women in the dress shops. "No, that's not for me," she says. "This one might be. I'll try on these three." No questions or seeking help here.

But she was strict with that cabbie, wasn't she?

Maybe some women have some kind of instinct for who is susceptible to what, or who is worth the effort. Jane seems to have a blank spot there.

Or it may have been that very instinct that made her so sure about answering Brian's ad. She may be learning, finally.

Her mother buys two of the dresses. They are soft and light, not unlike the outfits Jane has been getting for herself, although they do look different on a body that, Jane sees, is almost gaunt in middle age.

Even though her mother shops swiftly, apparently knowing just what she likes, it's getting late when she suggests lunch. "We'd better go pick up your little sister— Lydia? And what about her mother?"

"Lucy? Oh no. Anyway, I think she looks forward to having Lydia off her hands for a few hours. I'm not sure about Lydia, either. She's not very civilized sometimes, and she's only nine. It's hard to take her to a proper restaurant. Why don't I make you something back at my place and leave you there to rest while I take Lydia out? Then when I get back, maybe you and I could go out for dinner. Or order in."

"Certainly not. I don't feel a bit like resting, and I promised you a good lunch. If Lydia doesn't behave, we can always leave, but you know, when you were little, it was charming how you came through when it was clear we wanted you to."

Her mother smiles, rather gently. Jane is amazed.

"Oh my," her mother breathes, as they walk down the apartment corridor to Lucy's. Well, Jane tried to warn her, didn't she? "How do you do," she says to Lucy, and, shaking Lydia's hand, "I'm very pleased to meet you. I hope you're in the mood for a really good meal, because I'm taking you out for lunch." Why would she shake a child's hand?

Still, she seems to have done something instantly right, because Lydia, to Jane's amazement, gets herself properly dressed in slacks (not even jeans!) and a plain, uninscribed T-shirt, both of course bought by Jane some weeks ago. And she is quiet and polite, almost friendly, walking between Jane and her mother, down to the taxi. "I thought," Jane's mother says, "that since this is a special occasion for me, coming here and meeting you, that we might as well treat ourselves to a cab. What do you think, Lydia?"

"Neat."

And so, apparently, is the small French restaurant, with its linen napkins and silver cutlery and real flowers and, to Jane, outrageous prices. She has never been here before,

but has heard about it, of course. On a Saturday afternoon, after the main lunch hour, it is uncrowded.

"Probably, Lydia," her mother says gently, "it's not a
good idea to kick the chair. I think they're not all that
sturdy." As if this were the chairs' fault, and ordinarily
kicking furniture is fine.

"Okay. What should I eat?"

"What do you like most days?"

"Hamburgers. Chips."

"They won't have those, but we'll ask the waiter and
find out what comes closest. Unless you'd like to try
something different. Because, you know, it's always interesting to try new things."

Did she speak to Jane like this once? Jane doesn't
remember.

"What's this?" A small, not entirely clean finger points
at the menu.

Jane's mother laughs. "Probably not your best alternative to hamburger and fries, for one thing. That's French
for snails."

How does she know what's French for anything?
Where did she herself learn how to behave in small,
expensive French restaurants?

"Oooh, yuck." That high, awful voice, but laughing.
"Really? People eat *snails*?"

"Some people. Not me. Probably not you, either. How
about you, Jane?"

"I don't think so." Jane tries to smile at both of them,
and finds herself succeeding.

"Can you recommend anything? Do you come here
very often?"

"I've never been before, so I don't know. But everything's supposed to be good." She said that, didn't she,

that she's never been here before. The truth just slipped out, instead of the enhancing lie. How odd.

How dangerous, and potentially pathetic! What if the truth started slipping out all the time, and she found herself telling her mother, or Lydia, the waiter, or anyone for that matter, "No, I don't have boyfriends, I don't really have friends, either, but let me tell you my hopes!"

Jane and her mother order dishes involving unusual vegetables covered in unusual sauces. The restaurant rustles up frites and meat at least shaped like a hamburger for Lydia. "But there's no bun," she complains.

"That's because this is a good restaurant," Jane's mother tells her. "In good restaurants, meat doesn't come in buns."

Lydia accepts this from her. What would she have said to Jane? "How come you're Jane's mother?"

"How come you're your mother's daughter?" Jane's mother and Lydia grin at each other as if they've made a joke. If they have, Jane doesn't get it.

"What?" she asks, and they turn their grins to her.

Is her mother *too* thin? Is she pale under her rouge, or whatever makeup she's wearing—rather a lot of it, too? She must be tired, she's traveled so far and done so much today. She isn't young, after all. On the other hand, she's not old, either, fifty-six is hardly over the hill, and it's only because she's Jane's mother, and some days Jane feels a hundred years old herself, that it seems as if she must be ancient. What she is, Jane supposes, is in that hovering state of post-young, pre-old that probably goes on for at least a couple of decades.

When she was exactly the age Jane is now, she was having Jane. It ought to be a good age for having babies: grown-up and settled and certain.

"I don't like this," Lydia complains. Except for the frites, which she's polished off nicely.

"You've hardly tried it," Jane says. "Do you know what it costs? This is a very expensive meal, and I think you'd better eat it up." Lydia's expression starts shifting.

"Well," Jane's mother intervenes, "I'm the one buying it, and I don't mind whether you eat it or not, Lydia. It's too bad if you don't, because it looks awfully good, but it's no skin off my nose." She barely glances up from her own meal, and her voice is light and careless. Lydia looks startled, then resumes eating, slowly and without much enthusiasm, but eating nevertheless.

So not caring appears to be an effective technique with children, used wisely. Perhaps her mother used it unwisely with Jane, leaving the impression that she really didn't care.

It's disconcerting to have an inkling of wrong-headedness. Or worse, wrong-heartedness.

Jane hears Lydia telling her mother, with surprising enthusiasm, about their Saturday afternoon outings. "Mostly we go to parks because I really like playing, but we always have lunch. Sometimes Jane buys me things, too."

"Oh? What kinds of things?"

"Stuff. Clothes. Like this," and Lydia plucks at her chest, at the T-shirt.

"So you have a pretty good time, eh?"

"Oh yeah. Sometimes it's neat." This is not a sentiment she has shared with Jane. "Anyway, my mom gets tired, so she likes it that I get to go out even if she can't take me. And we don't have enough money, you know."

As if Jane does? Well yes, in comparison she does. But as if Jane doesn't have full-time work of her own, and also isn't apt to be weary on weekends?

"Also," Lydia is continuing in this peculiarly grown-up, chatty voice, "she says it means she has time to herself. She says she loves me, but it's nice when I'm out, too." That's certainly frank, isn't it? Doesn't it hurt Lydia's feelings, that Lucy's so grateful to have her out of her way? Perhaps the impact is blunted by love.

"Yes," Jane's mother says, "mothers do need time off. It's quite a tough job, you know."

Tougher, in Lucy and Lydia's case, than Jane's mother could imagine. Jane supposes she ought to have mentioned earlier what horrors lie in Lydia's history. Still, if they run out of conversation later this evening, it will be a story to tell.

Oh shameful, using Lydia's tragedies to entertain Jane's mother! Or to fill anticipated silences.

"If you want to take a cab back to my place, Mother," Jane suggests when lunch is finished, "I'll take Lydia home." Because lunch has gone on for an unusually long time, and there is now not a great deal left of Jane and Lydia's afternoon, she will not, thankfully, have to entertain the child further. Time's almost up.

"That's a good idea, I think I'll do that. Will you be long?"

"Just an hour or so. Lydia and I usually take the bus to her place. You could have a nap," she suggests hopefully. Or would it be better if her mother waited until they were alone, so there would be less empty waking time between them?

"I'll see. I may sit for a while, anyway. It has been a busy day."

Outside the restaurant, they head in different directions. Jane's mother again puts out her hand to shake Lydia's, just as if she were a grown-up. "It's been a real pleasure, Lydia. I hope we can get together again some day."

Lydia nods solemnly. "That'd be nice. Thank you for lunch."

"You're entirely welcome." They smile at each other, not like conspirators, exactly, but like people pleased with each other.

Today Jane returns Lydia right to her apartment door. If anything happened to Lydia because Jane had left her on the sidewalk, how would she be able to explain it to her mother? Not that anything would happen, but you never know. "I'll see you next Saturday, then."

"Sure. Will your mother be there?"

"No, she's going home tomorrow."

"Oh." Lydia sounds disappointed. "I like her."

"Yes, I noticed. She liked you, too." The child does have a smile like sunshine. She looks so pleased to be liked. "But I'll be here anyway, sweetie." They stare at each other, astonished. Actually, it feels rather nice; although what if Lydia came to count on it? Duty is difficult enough, without bringing affection into it.

And speaking of duty . . . with a sigh, she heads home.

"What a beautiful child." Instead of lying down, Jane's mother has taken her new shoes out of their boxes and draped her new dresses over the loveseat, and is regarding them. "She's going to be quite a stunner when she grows up. That hair—when I was younger I would have killed for hair like that. Although, of course, it makes getting the right clothes harder. It's more difficult to find just the right colors than if you have ordinary hair like you and me. Although even redheads can get away with a lot more than they could in my day."

As if her day is over. Likely it is, though. Even Jane's day felt pretty much over, until recently.

"Like my new clothes?"

"Very nice. Can't you get anything like them back home?"

"Not really. It's nice to have something different from what everybody else has seen a hundred times on the racks."

Oh vanity. So discouraging to have a vain mother!

"It's not really why I wanted to come down, though. I expect you realize that—you've always been a clever girl." There is that strange tone in her mother's voice again, that Jane heard on the phone the other night.

And if Jane's so clever, how come her mother has never particularly mentioned it before? Maybe she assumes that someone plain must be clever, that would be like her, wouldn't it. "Tea?" Jane asks.

"That would be nice. Then I'd like us to talk."

"Aren't you tired? I thought you might want to lie down."

"I can't afford to be tired." Jane is startled, and her mother looks startled, by the unexpected snap in her voice.

Her mother has something upsetting to say, then. And Jane thinks she can guess what it is: her mother has been hanging around with some man and they've decided to get married and she's come to break the news. How bad is news like that to Jane? Why would she care, especially?

"What kind of tea?"

"Anything. Any tea is fine." Her mother sounds irritated; that's more like it.

By the time Jane returns to the living room with the tray, her mother has cleared away the dresses and shoes and is sitting in the wicker chair across the coffee table from the loveseat. It's like a chairman's chair: the one the person in charge would naturally choose. It also means that whatever her news is, apparently it won't involve embraces, or reassuring pats on hands or knees. Her mother's red-tipped hands press on her knees as Jane pours. "Lemon?"

"Just plain." Her mother's nose wrinkles. "Whatever's this?"

"Herbal tea. I like it, don't you? I make it all the time." Because Jane, unlike her mother, is a sophisticated city woman who wouldn't dream of brewing ordinary tea in bags.

"Not much. It smells strange. Like a crop of something that's been in the barn too long."

"Sorry."

What does she see, watching Jane so closely? A daughter plain as tea? How many secrets does she know, or can she guess?

"Now then, Jane. This is difficult, and what I'd like you to do is let me speak my piece before you say anything. Can you do that?"

"Sure. I guess. If you want." How awful is this man, or how upset does her mother think Jane is going to be? But then, how abruptly abandoned Jane does feel, how alone in the world. This makes no sense; so many real things, however, make no sense.

Her mother smiles, taking the edge off something. "Now then. I'm sorry to have to be so blunt, but there's no particularly easy way to say this. I seem to have cancer. It started in my uterus but they're afraid it may have spread and gotten a bit out of hand. I'll be having more tests, and then likely surgery very soon, and then quite a long series of treatments and more tests. They sound hopeful." The lines in her face, however, are tight with terror.

Jane seems to have missed the real news. She's stuck back at the word uterus, so personal and also clinical, especially in connection with her mother. Both sexual and reproductive; neither a way she wants to think about her mother. But that's not the point, is it? She must try to catch up.

"Me, though," her mother is saying, "I think it's too late. I can feel it, I think. It's growing, and I don't know where it's gotten to, but it's in there eating away, and it's going to pop out again. I'd like to be brave enough to just skip all the treatments and let it take me, but it turns out I'm not, yet. Maybe I will be one of these days. Maybe dying will start to look good, I don't know. I think the end is going to be the same, though, whether I try or not. Oh, Jane, I'm not old! It feels so unfair!"

Unfairness, now there's a concept the two of them might profitably and cozily discuss. Something they might find agreement on.

But Jane, it seems, is speechless; still catching up with the words.

Her mother straightens. "Nobody else knows yet, except me and a couple of doctors, and probably," she smiles again briefly, "a few dozen nurses and technicians and therefore half the town. But theoretically, anyway, nobody knows. I wanted you to. I know how terrible it was for you when your father died. I don't know whether it's harder or easier when a death comes fast like that. I wish to God mine was coming fast." What a cry that is: of bitterness and fear. As if her mother's whole vision is filled by a terrible, thick, high, broad, stone wall into which she is being slowly, slowly pressed, preferring a head-on crash.

"Anyway, I had to come and tell you myself, not write you or mention it on the phone. This is," and now she leans forward, picks up her tea, "the hardest thing I've ever done. The hardest day I ever had was when they told me, but this is the hardest thing I've ever actually done."

What did she do when the doctor told her, the two of them alone together in his office? Dr. Hargety, probably. He has been her doctor for years, used to be Jane's, once was Jane's father's. He'd probably be gentle. Relatively gentle. He was good with Jane when she was a teenager seeking help for pimples. It seemed to her terrible enough to be plain, without getting a bad complexion as well. He gave her a prescription, which did the trick. He could have done nothing like that for her mother.

Her mother is going to die. This is a new idea for Jane. It has never occurred to her that this will happen.

How amazingly alone she is going to be; suspended drifting and untethered, in a universe of other people's lives.

But Brian. There's Brian, she'd forgotten for a moment, overwhelmed by immediate news. She has a good deal of hope, after all, especially compared to her mother.

Her mother is going to suffer. Jane has nowhere in her mind or heart to put that knowledge.

Her mother is looking at her, and Jane doesn't know what to say. She doesn't even know how to speak. She leans over and picks up her tea. Her hand, she sees, is as steady as if she didn't care. Her mother's hand, though, was also steady when she picked up her own tea, and she most certainly cares. So they seem to be two steady women, with something unexpectedly in common after all.

Obviously what her mother has come here to say is the truth. Fact. But what a peculiar thing reality is, terrible and cruel and apparently difficult to grip. This is the most real thing that has ever happened to Jane (as if it were actually happening to Jane, and not her mother), even more real than when her father died. They didn't have one of these moments, she and her father, sitting together and discussing what was going to happen. It just happened. So this is more real, in a way.

She ought to stand up now, go to her mother, bend over and embrace her. They should weep, or something. They should spend the rest of these hours talking, comparing, telling stories, wrapping up—something. Jane finds she can't move. Her mother doesn't, either.

What sort of daughter is she, anyway? Again her mother has demonstrated Jane's incapacity, inability.

The person Jane could talk to at this moment, whose shoulder she might weep into, would be Brian. She almost says it out loud: "If only Brian were here," just catching the words before they slip out. As if he could save both of them, a man handy in so many ways besides painting, or repairing small appliances.

She can write to him, that may help. He may have something comforting or wise to say, writing back. Meanwhile her mother, who doesn't dream of his existence, is dying, and Jane herself is frozen, paralyzed by the prospect of such a dramatic transformation. Her mother may be, also. At any rate there doesn't seem to be much either of them can do at this moment except what they're doing, which is to look sorrowfully and inadequately into their separate cups of tea, and at their similarly thin-skinned hands.

8

"Dear Jane,

"It was very nice to get your letter and so soon. I got some other ansers to my ad and so far I rote 2 but nobody who got back to me as quick as you. You must be a very kind person, do you rite other people to or just me?

"You were rite about the libary, I ast to work there and there letting me and so far its working out good. Its kind of quiet but I'll probily get use to that. I'm trying to read some things but its kind of hard, I'm not use to reading but mostly thats all there is to do because the libary isnt very busy exept for putting books on shelfs in order. Also some guys try to be there own lawyer in here so are always coming in wanting difrent legal kinds of books so I learn some things when we talk. Maybe I shud of done that kind of thing myself exept I never thot I was smart enough and now there is not much point since I dont have very much longer to be in here.

"Anyways some of the books I've looked at are intresting but the ones I like most are about stuff like fixing things, I mite try going into that line of work when I get out because I want to go straight this time thats for sure. So thanks for

121

the idea, it makes me think about you sometimes like maybe when I'm putting books away or getting them out for guys your doing something like that to.

"I wudnt of got this job exept the other guy that was doing it got out and they needed somebody and I ast at the rite time. Also its the kind of job they give a guy whos going to be getting out pretty soon. Of course you have to have a good record they dont put the hard cases in the libary, they have to work there tails off at hard jobs like laundry or cleaning up. I guess they like to keep them sweating so they dont have time for makeing trouble.

"The only thing I miss about the kitchen I guess is the other guys they were sombody to talk to but then theres people to talk to in the libary too like when a guy comes in and hes supost to be in for life for killing a bunch of people or something and hes looking for ways to get out legal ways I mean ha ha!

"So I've heard some intresting stuff that way I guess some crazy stories thats for sure!

"Hows your plans going for a union? Since theres just me in the libary here and I got to do pretty much what I'm told it doesnt look like thered be reason to have one here but maybe its a good thing outside. I never worked in a place that had a union tho so I dont know. Anyways what I figure is whatever sticks it to the bosses is good enuf for me.

"Did you mean it about makeing a sweater for me? If so arms 34 inch, chest 41 but it dont matter if its too big because I like sweaters big. If you mean it thanks.

"This has got real long and even tho I got plenty more to tell you about probily I shud stop now. I hope youll rite back to me soon because its real nice getting your letters! I promise I'll rite back.

"Do you know any books you think I wud like if so please tell me so I can see if there here. I am looking to improve myself espesialy with getting out soon. I figure theres stuff a guy ought to know on the outside because somtimes when your out there its hard to figure out by yourself and somtimes not knowing gets you in trouble even if you didnt ever mean to be.

"Now I really got to stop because this has got real long. Just so you know I been riting this in the libary so you can see I am putting my time to good use ha ha!

"Sinserly,

"Brian Dexter."

There, see?

Never mind the grammar, never mind the spelling, Jane's been right all along! That faith, feeling, whatever, she's had that he's going to be free turns out to be precisely right. *That's* what faith is, a firm knowing, resulting in reality.

Just for an instant Jane has a terrifying vision, but it speeds past her mind's eye so quickly she barely gets a glimpse. She certainly doesn't try to recall it, because really, the other picture's so much better, warmer. There are no ominous overtones to her sitting, all dressed up, made up and ready, on a straight-backed chair just inside the door to her apartment, listening to sounds, listening for footsteps. And those footsteps finally coming up and up the stairs, firm and steady and exciting.

What if—no, when—that happens?

"I dont have very much longer to be in here," he writes. And "I am looking to improve myself espesialy with getting out soon."

What is "very much longer"? How soon is "soon"?

She does, after all, feel another chill; just a little one, and then it's gone again. Anyway, this letter is real enough for the time being. Paper is plenty.

How odd it seems that he doesn't know about her mother. Of course she hasn't told him yet, but it still feels strange that even though they're so close during every moment of Jane's days (and nights), he is unaware of this huge and terminal event.

And of other vital matters, too.

Such as Jane's increasingly serious dreams of maternity. Sometimes, lying cozily in bed with Brian, she has heard a child cry out. "Leave it," he has urged sleepily. "It's nothing."

"No, I have to go," and she has seen herself pulling away from warm arms, and standing and moving quietly in the darkness to the child. They have even had minor quarrels on the subject, him impatient with Jane's concern. "For chrissake, there's nothing wrong with the kid, let her cry. It's good for her, makes her lungs big and strong. Like her mother's," and he'd grin and reach out for Jane.

Jane, too, would smile, but would get up to check the child anyway; because terrible things can happen to babies in a moment, and who could truly and seriously argue against taking care? Also it looks good, that she is so maternal. A man may resent this on occasion, but must also admire it. It must be something that is part of any man's picture of a woman he wants.

What about this letter, though? It's a tricky business, isn't it? It seems to say too much, in a way; more than she wanted to know. Brian Dexter exists in her life and he exists here on paper, and it's no simple matter to make those two existences hang together somehow.

She begins again at the beginning.

Dear Jane. They have become less formal: no more Dear Jane Smith. So that's good.

Why does he call everything nice? Once again he has found it "nice" to get her letter, and thinks she must be a very "nice" person.

Who are the two others he's written, and why did he? Are they also "nice"? Are they glamorous women with red-tipped fingers and glossy blonde hair? Slender and raucous, throwing their heads back to laugh at rude jokes? (Jane must see herself as the only "nice" person who would write letters to a prisoner.)

It seems she was wise after all to write him back quickly. It may have given her an edge over the two mysterious others.

It's grand that he has taken her advice and is now working in the library. Too bad he still can't spell it, and that he isn't fond of reading. It's good, though, to know he is considered well behaved. Frightening to think he is in prison (and, worse, alone in the library) with men who have killed. And who are, apparently, trying to get out.

She hopes those aren't the sort of men Brian likes to be friends with. Imagine coming home from work to find a bunch of his murderous cronies sitting around the place!

And with a child in the house!

If that is the case, she will have to be firm.

It's great that he likes to fix things. There are things that go wrong even in an apartment that it would be helpful to be able to take care of, instead of having to call the landlord and wait and wait for repairs. Even a simple matter like a dripping faucet is beyond Jane, although she has learned to venture down to the dark basement to change a fuse when the need arises. Men, even the ones who live in the apartment below, just seem to know how to do things like that. It's not as if they have to learn, or feel particularly daring when they undertake them.

Can Brian fix anything, from cars to refrigerators and toasters? Any of that could come in handy.

Like her, he is entertained by the idea of the two of them, miles and miles apart, doing the same tasks at the same time: shelving books, or checking them out for people. She is pleased he has that kind of imagination. She is glad he is grateful for her suggestion.

She is also pleased to learn that he can't be considered a "hard case," or he would never have been assigned the library job. Not that she ever imagined him a hard case, of course. Who dreams of brutal men?

Well, maybe some women. Not Jane.

She will look forward to hearing some of the "crazy stories" he has picked up from fellow inmates: those murderers (even multiple ones, apparently) trying to figure out ways to get themselves free.

Too bad he made those little jokes and then felt compelled to write "ha ha" to make it clear that he was kidding, but maybe he doesn't know she has a sense of humor and can get a joke without being nudged (which anyway isn't necessarily or always true).

It's one more thing she can correct—gently and kindly, of course—for which he will no doubt be grateful. That and his grammar and his spelling. He does, after all, seem to be a man who is willing to learn.

There are always happy ways of seeing things.

And here's another one: not all men, and she knows this from magazines and books, remember to ask a woman about herself. So it's a good sign, isn't it, when he asks about the progress of the union?

She is glad he is in favor of the idea, however clumsily he expresses his support: whatever "sticks it" to bosses.

It does appear he has some history of employment; at least he speaks of never having worked in a place with a union, and surely that implies he has worked in places without one? So he can't be unemployable, or lazy. He has only had unspecified troubles.

It's sweet that he wants to learn more so that he can get along better when he gets out. She wonders what efforts he made in the past (on his own, without Jane's guidance), only to find himself inadvertently in trouble again just because of not knowing what to do or how to act.

Clearly he has been in and out of jail more than once. There's not only that reference to getting in trouble again, but his pledge to go straight this time. As if he hasn't managed to go straight before.

Jane finds it more natural to think of his history in terms of mistakes, not crimes.

She tries to picture, from his measurements, his size, his shape. At least she now has numbers to work with: sleeve length, chest breadth. She can knit her heart out now.

So just look at all the information this letter contains, especially between the lines, which is exactly where Jane is skilled at deciphering.

He's getting out soon—isn't that exciting! What would he think of a child?

He likes a prompt response—well, so does she. She will write him, but not until she replaces her white writing paper with new stationery: something with a design, a spray of flowers, say. Better than scent, that will demonstrate to him there truly is a woman here, at this end of his correspondence. Who knows what temptations those other women resort to? Jane has so few weapons.

Is it odd that he hasn't asked her for a picture? It's certainly not a subject she'll be raising herself. But perhaps he's ugly: deformed or injured in some repellent way.

No. But even if he were, say, scarred by a knife, would she not enjoy tracing those lines with her fingers? Might a wounded man not be more compelling than a smooth and unmarked one? These are signs that a man has been alive, surely.

Jane feels almost fat with the fullness of everything, joyful and painful and grief-filled or confused, that's going on these days, as if parts of her body are starting to burst out of her clothes, a breast here, a thigh there. It feels as if she has begun to outgrow herself, not a very comfortable sensation, although she expects it's probably just a matter of getting used to it.

Time goes so quickly when a person's mind is busy. Where has the evening gone? It's hard to get to sleep.

In the morning, she puts his letter in her purse to take with her to work: like a talisman, it offers her its paper strength, so that she feels more powerful knowing it's there. At lunch time, in the staff room, she opens her purse to touch it surreptitiously: her glowing secret.

By now she can barely remember what it says, even though every word ought to be carved in her mind, or lit in neon. What remains is the main, real point: he's getting out soon.

What is he doing right this minute: having lunch, too? Drinking a chipped tin mug of bitter coffee, just as she's drinking a flowered ceramic cup of staff-room coffee, also somewhat on the bitter side? He may be far away, but there is every chance that at the hour she takes lunch, he does too. While she sits in this staff room listening to the laughter and conversations, is he not likely in some huge hall, filled with rows of long wooden tables, folding metal chairs, metal plates and plastic cutlery, a din of voices shouting and threatening (and laughing, as well?)—is that not likely?

She imagines him observing, listening. She imagines him waiting for the letter she will write tonight on the new paper she'll buy on her way home. She imagines him growing gentler from his hours in the library, those new surroundings providing a contemplative quiet.

She expects a good deal more from a prison library, doesn't she, than from the one in which she works herself?

Because he is, among so many other things, her friend, he'll know what to say about things like being an orphan, when she tells him about her mother. He'll be able to suggest how Jane might speak to her, or touch her, even how to think about her.

"I am looking to improve myself espesialy with getting out soon," his letter says. This she does remember: "I dont have very much longer to be in here."

Jane has so much exciting news, and one of these days won't she have some astonishing events to tell! Won't people be amazed, won't they stare at her, mouths agape. It's so delightful, all this delicious, secret knowledge, that she can't help smiling—probably rather foolishly, if anyone were looking.

9

The writing paper Jane selects is very slightly pink, with scalloped edges and the faint silvery outline of a rose at the top. The paper itself is dense, so anything written on it will seem both important and graceful. Like Jane's new clothes, this is a matter of marketing and packaging: a skill she is learning.

First, pay attention to him.

"Dear Brian,

"I received your letter, thank you very much, just yesterday, and was pleased to hear all your news. It's great that you've transferred to the library, and I hope if there are any books it doesn't have that you think it should have, you'll let me know. There are things like inter-library loans we could arrange. Also I'll be thinking about books you might enjoy."

Actually, she hasn't the faintest idea if the inter-library loan system applies to prisons. Also she rather hopes he doesn't bother her with small demands. For love Jane would happily do enormous things, but is less cheerful about little, irritating tasks. Still, it's the sort of offer that leaves a generous impression.

"I'm impressed that you enjoy fixing things. I'm not very good, myself, at things like that—in fact I usually find that how things are put together is a real mystery to me!"

Which should tell him he has abilities she would value. Also that she is not one of those briskly efficient women who can do anything, making their men feel extraneous and useless. Around Jane, Brian Dexter could be hearty and protective, wonderfully male. She hasn't an objection in the world to that.

"I, too, find it pleasant to think of you doing things in your library when I'm doing the same things in mine. Just today, in the staff room at noon, I was wondering if you were having lunch right then too, and what it was like. Is the food good?"

On the other hand, details might sharpen the vision too much; and mightn't questions be hurtful? She imagines he advertised in the first place to get word from the outside, not questions about his world inside.

And she does have so much to tell him, this dear friend, this close companion of her heart. Oh, if he were here, he would hold her with his sturdy arms, and she would stroke the fine hairs on the backs of his hands. His grip would tighten as he listened.

"You may think it's strange to get another letter so soon, when you just wrote yours, which I just received. However, several upsetting things have happened here, and I thought telling you would make me feel better. Or you could help me understand. I do feel you must be an understanding kind of man."

Daring. Still, there he is, her lover, friend, and confidant, her captive audience, comrade, enchanted prince-in-waiting, twin of her soul, her heart's missing piece. All that.

"Since I last wrote, my mother has been for a visit. She said it was to go shopping, but it turned out when she got here she had awful news. She has cancer, and is going to have surgery and other treatments, but she says she is going to die anyway."

Those are not many words, but he'll know how hard they were. Jane very nearly found herself unable to write the word "die."

When she put her mother on the bus for home last Sunday, they brushed cheeks with the same impersonality with which they had greeted each other. No tears, only brisk, stiff waves. What Jane could see was that however alone she has been in the world to this point, it's nothing to how alone she will finally be. Selfish and childish, of course, to be thinking only of herself, but what her mother faced didn't bear thinking about: real, true disappearance.

If Jane disappeared, she wouldn't even leave behind a daughter having selfish thoughts.

"I'm so sorry, Mother. I don't know what to say."

"That's all right. I know it takes getting used to."

How long, exactly? How much time would her mother, for instance, need to get used to the ideas, first of suffering, then of death? Decades, Jane would have thought. Centuries. There was her mother, riding back home on the bus, staring out the window beside her into darkness. Or seeing the reflection of her own thinning face. How cold she must have thought her tearless daughter.

There is very little point in saving tears for funerals. They don't do the dead much good then.

But maybe she was grateful to have been spared a scene. Maybe she needed all her strength to stay upright herself. She might have been pleased enough with a stoic, stern, reserved daughter.

"My mother and I haven't been very close," Jane writes, "but it came as quite a shock. I didn't know what to say. Has anything like this ever happened to you?"

Pretty personal question. What if he answers, crossly, "All I asked for was a few letters, not a lot of nosy questions."

Not her Brian.

"I never really thought of her being ill before, and certainly not about her dying. I guess that was foolish. I mean, my father died, so I should have known. I don't know how to explain this very well. It means I won't have any family left, for one thing. Do you have a family?"

She writes that question so swiftly there's no time to consider the possible answers.

"I guess I'm still confused, because I thought when she said she had something serious to tell me, she was probably getting married again or something. She's almost sixty, but still very attractive, and I know she has men friends." And from that, let him assume that in the matter of attractiveness Jane takes after her mother. "I guess that would have upset me too, but not like this. Also it's confusing when you think one thing is going to happen and then something else altogether happens and you're not ready at all. Do you know what I mean?

"It's funny, thinking about you when we haven't even met yet."

Yet. Will he hear the invitation and what she has in mind? "I have this idea that you know all kinds of things, and you'll say something that will make things clearer. I don't mean you *have* to do that, it's just this feeling I have."

These are the most intimate words she has written to him. Brave Jane. Because what if his dreams, unlike hers, have not included cozy evenings in a wicker-and-pastel apartment? What if he thinks, "What the hell is she talking about? What the fuck does she want?" and throws out her letter and never writes again.

Jane's black-inked pen races on. "My mother," she tells him, "has always been thin, but now she's looking kind of drawn-out and tired. I guess that happens a lot anyway to women who are thin and getting older, so it's probably not just being sick. It's hard to be close to her. Sometimes I think mothers should be fuller, do you know what I mean? So they'd be more comfortable. Also when somebody's hair is just so, and their makeup and everything else, you just feel you're going to mess them up if you touch them. That's one way we're different, I'm more casual that way, and rounder (I don't mean fat at all), so I figure I'd be easier to hug or whatever." For a child, is of course what she's talking about, but let him hear more if he can.

"I think she's always wanted me to be more like her in some ways, but I suppose a lot of mothers are like that. I left home after my father died, because I wanted to make something of myself." Really? What? "Of course I don't want her to die, and I certainly don't want her to suffer. But I don't want to give up my own life here, either, to look after her." As if anyone has asked her to. "Do you think I'm selfish?"

But what do people in prison understand about selfishness? Isn't it the very root of crime? He might not recognize selfishness if he tripped over it. As her mother might say.

Jane is surprised to hear her mother's voice this way, its small-town clichés in those small-town accents in Jane's head. What if, as her mother dies, her spirit and voice more and more take over? Well, Jane might begin to look with interest at men who wear white shoes and belts and add dark dabs of color to their hair. She might come to appreciate the slightly portly, crumpled-skin look of older men who still take pride in their appearance. She might learn bridge, and become relatively lively. She might find unfamiliar skills beginning to come naturally.

She might be surprisingly brave in ways she hasn't considered, although it has never seemed before that it takes much courage to live her mother's life.

She could become rail-thin, with an aptitude for a certain kind of glamor.

"Rail-thin" is the sort of expression her mother would use.

She might buff and shape and polish her fingernails. That would be easy enough, but what about the rest? In what ways, precisely, might her mother's spirit change Jane, overtaking her?

"I know you only get to send a couple of letters a month, but I'm hoping to hear from you soon. I hope you don't mind me writing all this to you."

There are already pages and pages here, but she is hardly finished. Now here's the point:

"You mention you expect to be getting out soon. Do you know when? I don't know if you feel like writing about what your plans are for then, but I'd be interested, of course." This strikes her as too detached, restrained.

"I don't know if you've ever been here, but this is a very pretty and prosperous city, and you might like to try it, unless you have definite plans elsewhere."

Deep breath now. Is he ready for this? For that matter, is she? She can dive in now, no hesitation or doubt, or she can stop right here. And nothing will happen, and nothing ever will change.

"Perhaps when you're free, we can meet? It is difficult, as I think you mentioned before, writing someone when you can't picture them." Although it has advantages. "Would you like to come and see me?"

There.

Now she would like to go on to say, "Come here to me, and I'll help you in any way you want, I'll take you in and comfort you and guide you, so you won't ever be in trouble again and we will live happily and passionately ever after, world without end, amen." Something like that.

She does see how frightening that might sound, coming out of the blue, in the mail.

Anyway, there's so much she still won't ask. The questions might include: Where are you from? What did you do to get where you are? Can you tell me who you are?

Family. What if, for him, family means wife and children, not merely parents and brothers and sisters? What if he is the husband of some loyal woman—or some faithless one, for that matter—and the father of youngsters who may be ashamed of him or love him, the way Simone loves Marcy or Jane's own phantom dark-haired child loves her? What if he has a whole life waiting for him, and no need for Jane?

Not possible. For one thing, if his life were so filled, he would have no need whatever for letters from strangers.

"Just to change the subject, plans for the union are going ahead, we've had one meeting, and more are planned. Did I tell you before that my friend Marcy from the library has a child?" No, of course she didn't. "She's a little girl, almost four, named Simone, and just the sweetest thing. I've come to simply adore her, and she's very fond of me, as well. I do enjoy children. Do you?"

Oh Jane, such lies!

Why stop now?

"I think children are very pure—do you know what I mean? Their affection is pure." Wasn't it children who called out "Plain Jane" at her in the schoolyard years ago? But Simone wouldn't be like that. All children don't have to be like that. Jane's own child, for instance, would be both kind and polite, she is sure.

"Perhaps when you leave where you are, if you decide to come here, you'd like to meet Simone. And my little sister, Lydia, I told you about her, didn't I? Do you like kids?"

It doesn't do to think too hard about that question, either.

"Oh, come here," is what she means. "Meet me, love me, live with me. Be my prisoner and I'll be yours."

Even if he's very tough and strong and self-assured and criminal, that might send him reeling into a corner of his cell. "Do write me again soon, and especially let me know your plans. I apologize if this letter seems disjointed, but I've been so busy lately, and upset, I find my thoughts just fly around." Don't they just! "I will look forward to hearing from you again soon. Please remember you're welcome to come here whenever you can. By the way, I'm well under way with your sweater—both sleeves are done and I'm working on the front. I hope you'll like it. I'm using quite a thick wool, so it'll be nice and heavy for winter."

She ends it, "All my best," and signs it, "Jane."

She would like to end it with, "Your most faithful and perpetual lover, who is waiting for you with eagerness you can't begin to imagine, Jane." But really.

There are so many pages that even with careful folding, the letter will barely fit into its envelope. She addresses it with great care—wouldn't it be awful if, of all their letters, this were the one to go astray?

She feels, sealing it and stamping it and heading out the door with it (because never mind that it's dark and late and who knows what is out there on the streets, this is urgent), that even though she's left out precisely her visions and intentions, he will know anyway. Like her, he will be able to read meanings as clearly by what's not said as by what is. Just as there are lies of omission as well as commission (and she's guilty of both in this letter, in the interests of a larger cause), there must also be truths of omission.

She is enormously relieved. All her troubles are now his, and she only needs to wait, and he will write and tell her everything. It's the sort of thing men are for, isn't it, lifting great heavy burdens from the arms of women and taking them up themselves? How wonderful, to have a willing shoulder for one's burdens. No wonder people prefer to spend their lives in pairs!

He will have answers to everything.

Even death? What might Brian Dexter know about death?

Her letter does contain some atrocious lies, doesn't it? Really, she might have been a paratrooper or marine, she is so skilled at camouflage. But her heart is intent on love, not war or death.

The lovers in books have such passionate lives! Their hearts are torn by separations, welded by the heat of reconciliations, are moved entirely by yearnings. Their hopes and thoughts are always with each other, love tops the list of their concerns. This is what love is, as far as Jane's concerned, so great a cause it surely justifies a few prevarications.

It's no longer warm outdoors; in fact there's a chilly breeze that seems to brush right through her skin. Still, the roots of her hair feel damp, and so do the palms of her hands and the backs of her knees, and beneath her arms and in the creases, what will someday be creases, of her forehead. It is odd and ill-feeling, to be warm and chilled at the same time.

It may be that her mother, that spirit of her mother's, is already on the move, making her sick.

Does the cancer make her mother sweat and shiver, or is it more a dull interior gnawing, reminding her of the sharp interior gnawing to come?

Jane really doesn't want to think about that. She wants to be in her bed, warm and curled up, watching him beside her, and also watching him far away, opening her letter, smiling at her words and being moved by them and then reaching for his pen to write her back. Things are happening, yes they are, events are on the move.

The night is not over. When she went out, the downstairs apartment was silent. Coming back, she hears raised voices: a quarrel, not a party.

"Son of a bitch!" she hears, and something glass smashes against a floor or wall. "I'm fucking fed up, give me a break, I'm getting the fuck out of here." And then a long and anguished "No, please!" and the thud of something heavy, a chair or a table being moved or turned over. She's never heard them quarrel before, Jim and Steve; but of course they must have their dramas. They must even have more dramas than most couples, since they face more difficulties. Maybe more than Jane, even.

But is this particular drama dangerous? It does sound violent. Should she knock on their door and offer to help, or just ask them to be quiet? Some hard object hits the door from the inside, making Jane flinch and step back. What if they killed each other? Then she'd be in the position of those people who sturdily ignore crimes going on right under their noses. "I heard them quarreling," she would have to say to the police, "and yes, I guess it sounded violent, but no, I didn't do anything. It wasn't any of my business, was it? What could I have done? That's what I thought, anyway." But she would be staring at the bloodied body of one or both of them.

She raises her hand to knock, but draws it back. She can't think of a single thing to say. And people have to get on with their own lives. Maybe it's even important to fight, although this outbreak does sound dangerous. Anyway, those two men make her uneasy at the best of times. Their customs, even their emotions, may be different from hers, and perhaps this sort of thing is more or less normal for people in their world. How would she know? They may not ordinarily behave like this, but perhaps it's not so odd.

"Bastard!" she hears. "You can't," and then the sentence is cut off.

She isn't one to interfere. She doesn't know how to interfere. Would someone else know what to do? Imagine those people who volunteer to work in crisis centers— how cautiously, but also how definitively, they must deal with tragedies. And how crisply they must be able to decide what is a tragedy, what a mere incident or temporary downturn.

What do they say to someone who calls and says "I've been raped" (as Jane herself might so easily have been, she now thinks, out mailing her letter so late and alone), or "I'm going to kill myself, I can't see any reason to live." Can you deal with that sort of thing if you haven't felt it yourself? How could someone inexperienced with certain passions know how to respond to, say, a threat of suicide?

Jane, for instance: however unhappy or merely tedious, her life has never looked better in the light of its own vanishing. Plainness is one thing, but blankness is incalculable.

Blankness is going to happen to her mother; eventually it will happen to Jane herself, ready or not. So can't she imagine choosing it (since it's hardly something a person merely drifts into)? There must be a terrible, blinding moment of thinking, "This is it, I have truly made up my mind."

But even if she got that far, how would she go about choosing a method? Slashed wrists? Hardly. Blood makes her queasy at the best of times, so no razor blades in a tub filled with water.

Are those men actually hurting each other, or just using furniture and words?

She would have no idea how to get her hands on a gun, nor would she be able to pull the trigger. She may have a plain face, but it hardly deserves to be splattered across the room.

Her apartment has no rafters from which to loop a rope. Anyway, even assuming it's done correctly and doesn't end in a slow, hideous dangling, hanging does result in swollen gaping tongue, bloated blue face. Muscles go slack, releasing the body's contents. Appallingly undignified.

The best would no doubt be some painless, gentle brand of pills that she could swallow and swallow, lying on her loveseat, a book propped on her chest, perhaps something enlightening playing on the television. She wouldn't have a clue how many to take of what kind of pills. It would be her luck to try something that would merely leave her retching and alive, or comatose, or brain-damaged in some especially gruesome way.

Anyway, she has perfectly splendid reasons to live.

Heavy fast footsteps are approaching the downstairs apartment door, startling Jane into running (lightly, softly) upstairs to her own door. There's more shouting now, in the hall she just escaped. "Fuck it," she hears, "you haven't been *listening*. If you won't even try, what do you expect? I've got to do this, that's all, but I told you, it doesn't have to be the end. It's your choice." Words are said in another voice Jane can't make out, and then the voice in the hall again. "Look, I can't change my mind. It's not like I decided something, I've *got* to. Oh shit, never mind. I'm out of here. I'll send for my things."

How furious he sounds—which one is it? The outside door slams.

Then there is a cry from below of such grief, Jane shivers from it. "Oh no, oh no, please don't go, oh God please don't go." Then more softly, "Oh don't go, please don't go." How much sorrow can there be? Jane feels pain in her own chest. Cautiously she peers down the stairs.

It's Jim down there. Steve must be the one who is gone, unless she's mixed them up. Jim is on his knees. His knees! Isn't he afraid someone will see him? He's on his knees, with his head in his hands, kneeling in the big hallway between his apartment door and the tin side-by-side mailboxes on the opposite wall. "Oh God," he is saying, "oh God."

Well, she can't just close her door. Violence she might not interrupt, but this—she can *see* him. It's not possible to misunderstand sorrow, or turn away pretending that it's nothing.

How would she sleep?

"Jim?" she calls hesitantly. "Jim? Are you all right?" Stupid question. But it makes him look around, take in the fact of his lack of privacy, look up to see Jane, clutching her sweater, at the top of her stairs. Embarrassed, she can see that he's embarrassed, he stands, brushes down his clothes, smoothing the tucked-in blue shirt, the gray cords. He has a lovely narrow body, wide shoulders, slim hips, long legs. She shouldn't have to write men in distant jails with such beauty just below.

"Sorry," he says, but his voice cracks. "Just a fight. It'll be okay. I'm sorry if we disturbed you."

"That's okay, I just came in." As if she couldn't have heard any of what went on before his pleading moments in the hall. "It's not that you disturbed me. I was going to make tea, would you like some?" She hadn't any idea of making tea. She would have gone to bed, but it doesn't matter so much.

"I don't know." How weary he sounds.

"I had a hard day, too," she hears herself saying; whereas really, she had quite a pleasing one, in a way. "Come on up."

"All right. You're very kind." He climbs the stairs like an old man: slowly, and as if he can't quite tell where to put his feet down next. He's not as handsome as usual. He has narrow fine features, but tonight they are drawn, and he has lines at the sides of his eyes and his mouth. She has read that appearances are very important to homosexual men, that they depend more than most on their looks.

She supposes she wouldn't be much more successful as a homosexual than as she is. Although perhaps homosexual women are different from men, and don't put such stock in looks.

Like suicide, she has never dreamed of women. It's hardness she wants, muscles and skin, not any softness like her own.

How does this sort of thing happen? She looks at him curiously. She has never been with him, with either of them, alone before. What on earth can she say?

144

Joan Barfoot

"I have camomile, is that okay?"

Jim is settling on her loveseat. "That's fine. Thanks."

He will have time, while she's in the kitchen, to pull himself together. She worries he might be weeping—that's what she'd be doing, she imagines, if a lover slammed out on her like that—but she wouldn't know what to do about tears from a man.

But he's dry-eyed when she returns. "Here," she says briskly, "it just needs to steep for another minute or two. I do like camomile, especially when I'm not feeling well." As if tea could actually heal anything more serious than, say, mild cramps. She sits in the chair opposite him.

"I'm sorry," he says again. "We didn't mean to disturb you."

"You didn't, don't worry. I was out. I just got in. I only really heard the door slam, so I looked out." She imagines this is another one of those worthwhile, comforting sorts of lies. "I was out mailing a letter. I have this man I write to." Would she spill her life, to save him spilling his? Keep a grip on yourself, Jane.

"You're lucky." Is that irony in his voice, or bitterness? "I guess you gathered Steve's walked out. Left me. I was upset. I guess I made a scene down there."

"It's only a scene if people are watching." This sounds so wise and almost existential, Jane is impressed with herself.

"Yeah. Maybe an audience of one doesn't count." He means her—he accuses her of watching, listening, an upstairs busybody? Have they made jokes? Oh, she feels crimson.

"Do you know how long we've been together?" How would she? As long as she's been here, but really, she has preferred to know nothing about them.

145

"Ten years. All my grown-up life. I've only ever been with one other guy. I met him at a party and we've been together ever since. What am I going to do without him?"

"Is he older than you?" Perhaps she should have used the past tense, as if Steve were dead; but anyway, what difference does it make how old they are?

"Five years. He's thirty-six. He did a whole lot of things before we got together. I guess now he'll be doing them again." He sighs. "He says he's bored, can you imagine anybody saying anything crueller than that?" Actually yes, she can, but doesn't say so. "Honest to God, I just felt comfortable, I didn't know he was bored. I thought it was nice getting dinner every night together and washing up and talking and going out to movies and plays and having friends in—I *like* being ordinary. He says he wants to go to bars. He wants to see different people and try differ-ent—things. I hate that. And it can kill you. I just wanted us to have our life."

Well, Jane certainly understands Jim's point of view, who better? How peculiar that achieving ordinary, settled life can make some people restless, even restless enough to leave. "I know what you mean," she says.

He looks at her, for the first time with some attention. "Do you?"

She shrugs. "Sure." How can she best express the vir-tues of ordinariness? "Just to know certain things are in place, so you can get on with your life and know it's solid—yeah, it makes sense to me, wanting that."

She may not be exactly eloquent, but at least she's managed to say something personal; even somewhat re-vealing, if he were listening and interested. Perhaps it's because he can't do anything for her, could never be the object of any of her hopes, that it's oddly relaxing, sitting here with him.

Although not for him, of course. For him, all this is terrible. "I don't know what to do without him." There are tears in his eyes. She does hope he isn't going to cry. "I've never been alone before."

"It's not so bad," she says with as much brisk confidence as she can manage. "I live alone, and it's not so awful. It's good to know how to look after yourself."

"I guess so," he says doubtfully. "It's just, I can cook and clean and write cheques and make a living, all that shit, that's not what I mean. It's being *alone*." Alone, he means, the way she is: in the evenings, in the mornings, in the kitchen, in bed, in every movement she makes in every moment in this place.

Not for much longer.

"Alone," repeating something she's read, "isn't the same as being lonely. It's a shock, of course, but once you get used to it, I bet you'll find there are good things. Like not being responsible to anybody. Or *for* anybody. Your time's your own. Things like that." Where *did* she read that?

"I don't want my time to be my own. I want it to be ours, his and mine. Like it's always been." He sounds like a child now, demanding his own way despite the opposing will of grown-ups.

"I know, I know." She tries to sound soothing. "Anyway, maybe he'll be back. Maybe right now he's thinking what a mistake he's made."

"Do you think so?" This time his face is lit with hope. He knows as little of her as she does of him, and may imagine she knows about these things.

"Why not? If it's been ten years for you, it's been ten years for him. It's hard for both of you, I would think." Ten years! This man here—however peculiar she may have considered his household—has had a ten-year

147

romance, something she has only dreamed of. It's not fair. Why should odd men be able to have what she's never had?

She would give her soul for ten years with Brian Dexter.

If she had a romance starting now, right this minute, and it lasted ten years, she would have a decade of talk and laughter and meals and movies and love—ten years of love! And if it ended then, she'd be thirty-eight, and surely she wouldn't care so much? Thirty-eight is old for this sort of thing, it must be, surely. But she'd have had it, she would have had ten years of what she wanted.

Then, maybe, she'd find something else to want. Because at thirty-eight, what difference could it make?

She would give her soul for ten years of romance.

"Anyway," she says, "even if he doesn't come back, you've already had more than a lot of other people. Nobody can take ten years away from you."

"Yeah, maybe. But that doesn't help right now."

Well, what does he want from her, then? If she isn't a help, why doesn't he just go off to his lonely bed and let her get to hers, so much more interesting now? It's almost midnight, and tomorrow's a work day.

He looks at his watch. "Oh God, I'm keeping you up, I didn't know it was so late. Thanks for the tea. And for taking care of me. That was kind, you know. Not everybody would have tried to help that way." He smiles, and it's such a nice smile, the little sad corners of his mouth struggling upward—he really is making an effort to be grateful. Her heart softens. She has such an immensely soft heart. Why does he have to be gay?

If he weren't, she could take him into her bed and wrap her warm arms around him and make all his sorrows go away.

He stands. "Maybe I'll be able to return the favor sometime. Not that I wish you anything awful, but you know, if you do need anything . . ."

"Thank you." She takes his hand. If he weren't gay, she'd never dream of taking his hand like this. "If you can't sleep, just knock on my door. Or tomorrow. Feel free. I'm here, and we're neighbors, after all." Surely the first time neighborliness has crossed her mind.

"You're so kind." He's very formal. "It's funny, I thought I had a lot of friends, but you're the one who was on the spot tonight. I appreciate it."

"If I hadn't been here, you'd have called someone, I'm sure. It's only that I was here."

Who could she call, if she had some tragedy?

Well, now she could call Jim downstairs. He said so. He doesn't know a thing about her, except what he may have noticed of her comings and goings, and probably he hasn't been especially interested, but now—they may be friends, sort of. She's not sure just what friendship is, but perhaps it's something to do with complementary needs.

How very full of incident of one sort and another her life has recently become. And how chock-full of feelings, not all of them her own.

At the door he turns—he's quite tall, much taller than she is—and smiles down at her. "Thanks again, Jane. I don't know what I'd have done tonight without you. It was nice of you to listen." Then, astonishingly, he reaches out and wraps his arms around her. He holds her for quite some time: several seconds. His shirt is soft; his chest is hard. She can feel his heartbeat. She can smell his faint aftershave. His arms are muscled. Her head fits nicely beneath his chin. She can feel how wide his shoulders are.

So this is what it's like, being embraced: as fine and solid and strong as she has suspected. She could stand forever, here in this grip.

Pity he steps back finally, and smiles again, and leaves. Pity he's so beautiful and perfect, but quite beyond Jane's grasp. Pity he's not Brian Dexter, for whom there are no guarantees at all of beauty or perfection.

10

Now the pace, like so much else, is heating up. "Dear Jane," she reads. How quickly he's answered her this time. It's true, then, she can count on him. The letter goes on:

"I was real sorry to here about your mother and I hope shes rong shes dieing. All I can think to say is everybodys got to go somtime and I dont know if that will make you feel better, its just getting use to it I guess.

"It kind of feels funny you thinking I cud say somthing to help, I dont know what, also its hard just riting. Maybe it wud be easier if we cud be talking.

"Well I have a suprise for you about that too, I hope you meant in your letter you wudnt mind meeting me because I'd like to meet you. The suprise is I guess I forgot to say before when I get out of here, 17 this month, I guess I been thinking about it so long so I didnt think to say the date.

"You ast me what I hope to do and I dont know yet exept for going straight and I mean to do that but its hard to think about more than just getting out and I guess I'll have to wait and see exept I wud like to go see you if you meant what you said. Like you say its hard to talk in letters its funny to know sombody and not know them too

151

(exept I know you must be a very nice person but I all ready told you that before.)

"Maybe you dont really want to meet me and if so just say so. I guess I shud say more about myself so you can say. So anyways I been here a long time, 10 years and I'm 38 years old, I had lots of trouble in my past but now like I say I'm really hoping to be finish with all that. What I want mostly is just to have a home and no more trouble thats all thats in my mind for getting out. I was kind of wild before but now I'm older things are difrent, like when I was a young guy I didnt think much about settling down but now just being in a quiet place is about the best I can think of. I guess I think about you having that kind of life so if you really mean I cud go see you thatd be great it gives me somthing real to look forward to not just getting out.

"I guess we havnt rote a whole lot of letters but its like I know you pretty well do you feel that way too even if I havnt told you a whole lot? Anyways I see us sitting around and getting to know each other better and you sound like a nice person so likely it wud be easier for me to be nicer too.

"The last days are hard, I thot theyd be easy knowing its close to the end but there really long and its strange but there even harder than when your a long way from getting out. Like I cant think about anything exept getting out but theres still guys bugging me about this and that and the same old work to do and the same old routins when it seems like everything ougt to be getting easier. But anyways I guess I'll make it because itd be dum to get mad about somthing now espesialy if you dont mind me visiting, let me know if you dont want me to but if you do I was thinking if I get out of here early on the 17 I cud get a train and be at your place by nite, of corse if I dont get out til later it mite be next day, so wud that be OK? I dont mean to bother you and if you dont want me to come just let me know but I thot if you really meant it it wud give me somthing to do rite away when I get out. If youve changed your mind dont worry, just they say here its good to have a plan or else you can get screwed up rite away as soon as you get out. See if you been in a long time its like everythings difrent and they say its hard to catch up and get use to things and thats when a guy can really get in trouble again which is what I definitly dont want to do.

"Can you notice my spellings better than before, also the words I use I hope. I been really studying and trying to improve myself working in the libary, I look up a lot of things in the dictionary exept some words I cant find, do you think its kind of weerd that you have to know pretty much how to spell things if your going to look them up? I know your really smart and I wudnt want you to be disapointed. I cudnt ever be as smart as you likely but I can try to get better. I guess you can tell I didnt go far in school but I dont think that has to mean I'm dum so I been reading and trying to remember about spelling.

"I guess after I visit you (if you still want me to!) I'll have to start looking for a job. Somtimes thats hard because a lot of people dont want to hire excons but I'm not going to give up, I'll just keep trying till I find somthing. Thats somthing else that happens somtimes, guys cant get a job very easy and they get tired of looking and do somthing dum and end up back here, but not me this time!

"If you hear of any jobs wud you let me know? I think I told you I'm good with my hands espesialy with cars and such. I use to be able to fix just about anything. I guess cars have changed some since I been here but like I said

I'm not dum so I shud be able to catch up pretty quick, I dont care much really where I live I mean what city or where in the contry even so long as I can work and keep my nose clean. But like I say if you changed your mind and dont want anything to do with me thats OK too, you dont have to, somtimes people say things they dont really mean even if they think they do so its OK if you dont any more, just let me know OK? If I dont hear difrent I can try to be at your house on the 17, evning, but dont worry if I'm not there it mite be next day like I said.

"You can phone here and leave a mesage for me if you need to, I can even go to the phone myself somtimes but not always so if I cant just leave a mesage. You are very nice, not everybodyd spend time riting a guy who hasnt done very much good in his life. If you dont want to see me like I say thats OK but I want you to know anyways that its been nice knowing you and it helped me to get your letters and have sombody to rite to, I wish I'd thot of it a long time ago!

"Everybody here is jealus because of me getting letters from you and also because of me getting out and maybe having somplace nice to go, at least to start out. Its like good things they dont have, maybe thats why there bugging me more.

"Anyways its soon! Like I said I'm sorry about your mother but we cud talk more about it maybe? Hopeing this finds you in good health and hapines I am,

"Your faithfull penpal,

"Brian (Dexter)."

Oh God.

Here's a date, a time: a week Tuesday evening, or a week Wednesday morning. Here he comes. Jane's hands tremble. Now what will she do?

A week from Tuesday, he may be on her doorstep. He may be sitting right across from her here, or beside her on this loveseat. There is that picture of herself, waiting, sitting quiet and still on a straight chair just inside the door, listening for his arrival, the door below clicking open, then shut, and the steps on the stairs. That first glimpse by him of her, by her of him. Herself softly dressed and him brimming with desire; their whole lives ahead of them, just waiting to be discovered.

Oh God. What on earth was she thinking of?

What has she done?

Somewhere in a place hundreds of miles away, where she's never been, there is a real Brian Dexter. A man she hasn't met spent some time painstakingly setting down these words she's been reading. There is a person who, after reading her earlier letters, actually asked to work in the library instead of the kitchen. Now he sits at a desk and talks to men who have murdered, and done other things, too. He must have pictures in his mind of violent or sordid acts. There is a real Brian Dexter, with real skin and true lines in his face and actual hairs on his chest, and his arms, and his legs.

There is a man coming here, to her small, safe, and private home, who is an utter stranger.

What has she done?

It can't be too late to stop all this. He says he'd understand. Surely that's a hopeful sign. If he's so understanding, there's no reason to be—what, startled, unnerved? Neither word comes even close.

But surely he can be, after all, the man of her vision. He can be both that and real, too. A vision made flesh. But anyone might change her mind at this point, there's no reason to be frightened. He knows. He would certainly forgive, he says as much.

So is she frightened of her Brian? Well, not of *her* Brian, no. Maybe just a bit, though, of that other man, the one who gets out of prison a week Tuesday, the thirty-eight-year-old man with "lots of trouble" in his past. He might, having suggested she should know something about him, have been a little more specific.

Still, is this not the friendliest and most open, not to mention most grammatical (if not, after all, the best spelled) of his letters? He intends to go straight, it is almost possible to *hear* his determination to go straight. He sounds as if Jane might be his only chance.

That's quite a responsibility.

But wasn't it precisely her intention?

How stupid of her to have absorbed the date and time of his release the way her mother may have listened to the doctor: she's been having such an interesting and pleasing life, and it's coming to an end. Unlike her mother, of course, she knows precisely when that will occur. And unlike her mother, she knows another life will follow.

There's no telling, though, if it will also be pleasing. All it is for sure is unknown. A blank in her immediate future, that at least is like her mother.

As he points out, everybody dies, the only questions are when and how. No big deal, maybe.

Hardly the tender, wise advice she was hoping for. "Everybodys got to go somtime" is scarcely consoling.

This is awful. This is a letter from her Brian, and it's sweet and open (barring his reticence on the actual subject of his actual mistakes) and as good as spells out his need for her. Okay, maybe she would have wished for words that were more polished and romantic, but still!

Who does she think she's been writing to, Fred Astaire, Cary Grant, those polished favorites of old movies on

Saturday-night TV? She has been writing to a prisoner named Brian Dexter, who's had none of their advantages. There are no cameras rolling, and he's not working from a script. These are his own words, and at least, as he once pointed out, he speaks "sinserly."

In a story, in *her* story, she would be so excited! She would barely be able to wait. She would already be cleaning her apartment and making plans for meals and deciding on flowers and getting out candles, ready to be lit. She would be regarding her body, feeling arms, imagining hipbones and thighs.

What if he comes to her door and looks at her and thinks, "She lied"? What if that puts him in a rage?

He might, feeling betrayed, strike out at her.

Not her Brian.

But perhaps she would deserve it. She can't even remember all the glossy, glamorizing lies she's told him. Whatever was she thinking of?

Oh, she would greet him with her hands covering her face.

How little, it turns out, she knows about him. This man is coming to her home and she doesn't even know how he's likely to behave, if he's volatile or patient (though he does sound patient, doesn't he?).

But isn't it magic, that he's really coming! And if that much is true, surely there's every chance the rest is, too. She's made one thing happen, and that must be a good sign.

Anyway, whatever he did before, and whatever he used to be like, he's older now. Maybe he doesn't come right out and say he's sorry for whatever it was that happened, but there's certainly regret when he writes, "I was kind of wild before but now I'm older things are difrent." What more could she want (besides better spelling)?

Everyone has wild oats to sow.

Perhaps he is Jane's.

Already she does feel somewhat wild. Other people when they're upset, they shout, or drink, or hit. Jane feels a little inclined to violence at the moment, and wouldn't mind having something to punch: a wall or a pillow or even a person, even herself.

How weak she must be; this wavering would never occur to a true romantic heroine. She is faithless compared with the sturdy devotion of the women in her novels. So perhaps after all she is undeserving: of love or life or any benevolent results at all.

No. She has done some good things, and really only a few bad ones. She must deserve something, some return. What else have all those Saturday afternoon hours with Lydia been for?

Read his letter again, Jane.

Really, what sweetness and hope! He is, and not just between the lines, making promises: to work, to be good. He expresses the thought that he might learn something about goodness and generosity from her. He sees that she can make him a better person. Is that not compelling, and exactly what she intended?

Anyway, criminals do tend to lose energy and become more placid, less dangerous, as they age: she has read that. It could be just as he says: that older, he is wiser, wanting different things. "Just being in a quiet place," he writes, "is about the best I can think of." Being in a quiet place, with a quiet person, is exactly what she wants, and what she has to offer. How much more compatible could they be?

Brian, who is good with his hands, will make a good living. Or he will once they persuade someone to hire him.

Will? Has she decided, then?

All this is terribly tiring. Like many mythical women, Sleeping Beauty, say, or (more ominously) Goldilocks, she'd like just to go to sleep, to wake up to something simply *done*. Miracle or disaster, as long as she missed the difficult part: deciding.

Who could she go to for help, or advice? All this is hard to explain at this point. Not Marcy, who would no doubt be baffled by how Jane got herself into this spot. Nor her mother, who has her own problems and anyway might think it was just another of Jane's stories. Or lies. Jim? She is so close to Jim she could almost reach down her hand and touch him. They might hold on to each other. They did have one pleasing embrace, although of course it was not the real thing, which would be much, much more, although also quite possibly more demanding and dangerous.

What does Brian think of gay men? He must know some in prison. Oh, she hopes he's tolerant, that he will understand about Jim, who may be her friend.

It's hard to understand that she actually, truly has to be concerned about any of this. It's hard to believe that Brian is not only real but is really coming here unless she stops him. It's hard to see how she can put together the tenderness of recent months with the upheaval ahead; not to mention this awful, betraying sense of menace.

The sweater's already so big. Imagine the man who would fill it! What chance would she have?

It's not fair, that this one brave and whimsical adventure, which has given her such pleasure, could turn out to be so difficult. When her intentions had such purity, and her longings were so ordinary; when all she really wanted was to be touched, and regarded with love, and also not to feel so awfully plain.

Whatever has she done?

11

Willy-nilly, despite all Jane's most careful construc-
tions, the world is moving in on her, apparently
dispassionately. Or, in a way, compassionately. Doing its
duty to her the way, perhaps, she took on Lydia: a mini-
mal execution of a social duty, hand-washing to follow.
"We did what we could" may be the best that anyone can
hope to say at the end of the day. And after that, well,
whose responsibility must the outcome be?

So when Jane's telephone rings tonight, it's the world
calling: poking its finger inquiringly, benevolently, into
her affairs. Mind you, she opened this small space herself,
when she set out on her pen-and-paper adventure. She
has no one to blame but herself.

How her nerves leap! Answering, she feels out of
breath, as if she's been running. Brian, released early? Or
her mother, breathless herself, saying, "You'd better
come, Jane, I've gotten terribly sick, there's no time left"?

An unfamiliar male voice. "Is this Jane Smith?" Brian?
It sounds a pleasant voice.

"Yes." Or someone selling carpet-cleaning services.

"Miss Smith, I'm from the city police. I hope you don't
mind the intrusion, but I'm calling in regard to Brian
Dexter. You know his name?"

Does she!

"What about him?"

"Well, this is a little awkward, but I wonder if you and I could arrange a chat about the situation. My name's Dave Barnes, by the way. Sergeant. We understand you've been corresponding with him, and frankly, we think it might be a good idea if you knew a little more about him. I believe you're aware his parole hearing was three months ago, and he'll be out shortly?"

No, she didn't know about the parole hearing. Three months ago is approximately when she saw his ad in the newspaper. Jane has no head for facts, but that's one.

Who is this "we" of whom this man speaks? Who has sat down and decided it would be a good idea for her to know more about Brian Dexter? Not to mention why.

"When?" she asks.

"Any time that's convenient for you."

"But I don't understand, do you always do this when somebody's being released?"

"Sometimes, in certain circumstances. The fact is, I'm sure you know prisoners' mail is read by authorities there, and there was some concern you haven't been told everything you might want to know. It's kind of a favor to you, really."

Jane was worried about people finding out, and then putting incorrect interpretations on events: that Marcy, say, or her mother, might judge her correspondence pitiable or amusing. She has understood it will take time, perhaps careful explanation, but most of all actual demonstrations of devotion to prove how accurate her intuition—whim?—has been. (Not everyone would see all this as a miracle. She is ambivalent at the moment herself, for that matter.)

And now it is brought home to her with this telephone call that (although she knew this in a vague and theoretical way) total strangers have been reading her letters and his, possibly laughing, apparently worrying, knowing secrets, or things they think are secrets. Strange eyes have been peering into her life.

Now strange men want to come right into her apartment and sit on her furniture and tell her things she probably doesn't want to hear.

A man, at any rate. A policeman. Someone obviously not on Brian's side.

And what is this Sergeant Barnes seeing as he sits in a busy police station, perhaps in an office of his own—who does he think he is talking to? Oh, what have her letters said, and more important, what have they implied? Some frantic old maid, desperate for a touch? Does he picture her older than she really is, more gray and pathetic? Just who does he think she is?

"It wouldn't take long, and we could do it any time. At your convenience, really. I'm working noon to midnight this week. There ought to be an hour in there you could spare."

"I don't understand, I don't see why you're going to all this trouble. Whose business is it if I want to write letters to somebody?" She would feel prouder of herself, pressing him, standing up for herself, if her voice didn't have this edge.

Does she even have a choice here? It hardly seems possible to resist the demands, however gently expressed, of a policeman—would it even be criminal, like resisting arrest? But more: how could she dream about Brian? How comfortable would she feel tonight curling up in bed tracing Brian's features in the darkness, feeling him trace hers? How could she picture their split-level house and their laughing child and the life they'd all have caring for each other? How could she picture his burly big body as a comfort and protection, with this policeman's words now lodged in her head?

Although he really hasn't said anything, yet.

Anyway, what do they (whoever they are) have against Brian? They're letting him out, he's paid his debt, he's even gotten a job in the prison library, and he's written to her of his intentions to get work, go straight, not fall again to crime (whatever his crime may have been). They must know all that, having read his letters. And hers. Oh God, her last letter, page after page about herself, her mother, so personal.

It's not their business, any of this. Even if she's been a bit frightened, it shouldn't be their business. This police-man has knowledge he should never have had. She knows nothing about him, and he will know all about her.

No wonder Brian's letters have been so cautious. He would know exactly the men who would be reading them. Now it makes even more sense how unspecific and even, well, sort of dull, they have been. Obviously she was intended to see more in them than was there. As she did, of course. He must have known he could trust her to interpret his true desires.

All right, then. She will be bright, unshakeable, firm, worthy of Brian's faith.

"All right, come when you like. Tonight, if you want." Whatever he has to say, she will hear without expression. Much of what he says will no doubt be lies, exaggera-tions. Brian has trusted her to know things, and she will know them, however hard this policeman tries to make her weaken, for whatever reason. This will be a test. She'll be able to tell Brian how she stood up for him. Not many couples have the opportunity for such a display of solidarity.

"Terrific. I can be there in an hour, okay?"

An hour! Always events come too swiftly. And people take her at her word. Why are they all, like this man, like Brian himself, so awfully literal?

She will make tea. Would he prefer beer? But he'll be on duty, and she has no beer. That's a man's drink. She could offer him wine.

She'd better get in beer for Brian. She doesn't imagine he's a man who'd care for herbal teas. She doesn't even know, though, what kind of beer he likes. She understands there are differences, but not exactly what they are.

Perhaps the sergeant can advise her.

Oh dear, he's on his way, and he's going to sit right here and force her to hear something he thinks will be good for her. Bad-tasting medicine, to cure her of something. Presuming an illness, when she has foreseen a healing. Healer.

Too bad Brian can't watch her triumphant resistance. How devoted he would have to feel, in view of her astounding loyalty.

Then he'd have to be loyal to her, and there'd be no reason at all to be scared. If she were scared.

It's interesting, tidying and clearing away for a man, even this one. He'll be big, because policemen aren't puny, and he'll likely have some air of authority.

When he goes, will he leave behind some residue of maleness? And when Brian comes, will he know there's been that presence?

It may make him more alert to how much he ought to care for her, knowing that other men have been here.

Jim, too, what sort of presence did he leave behind him? Some other kind of scent for Brian to detect?

What if all any of them can smell is loneliness, or despair?

They will smell flowers. They will smell lightness and grace. In the bathroom, she does her best to draw her hair around her face, bouncing it outward for a carefree effect. She draws a line of blusher with a brush across her cheekbones. She freshens her lipstick, and tucks in her blouse. Lifting her head seems to lift her whole body. She thinks she looks like a proud woman, no one to be fooled with.

Here comes the world now: a light knock, no pounding of an official fist. He isn't so large. Nor is he in uniform. He's even almost handsome, if she especially liked very short hair. (She could like short hair, she could like long hair, she could grow partial to no hair at all, if need be.) He has a neat, even mouth. His blue eyes, though, look too small and close together. He doesn't exactly tower over her, although he's tall enough. He is wearing beige slacks, a dark brown shirt, dark brown shining leather shoes. His hair is brown, too, with hints of gray. Except for his eyes, he is a study in various shades of brown. He isn't bad-looking at all.

Who knows, once this starts, where it will end? If she lets him in, who knows who will follow: a parade, an unstoppable column of catastrophe appearing at her door, demanding admission?

Melodramatic, no doubt.

"Come in," she says. "I've made tea." She gestures toward the chair. He'd probably sit there anyway, since it seems to be the place people who want to be in charge choose automatically. "Unless you'd like a drink? I have wine." She sounds too anxious, a fretful, nervous hostess. Let him take what she gives him, this wasn't her idea, and he isn't her idea of an invited, chosen guest. Although he is attractive.

What does he see? When she was assessing him at the door, he must have been doing the same to her. What if he's thinking, "Oh well, that explains it. Poor thing, no wonder she had to write to a stranger."

He isn't even looking at her, really. "Tea sounds fine." He just sounds ordinary. What extraordinary words is he waiting to say? Has he planned them? Is he changing any of them, now that he's met her?

She supposes it's too late to say, "I've changed my mind, I'd like you to go. So leave, please." He's gone to some trouble, after all. There's such a thing as simply being rude.

He needn't think he or his words are welcome, though. She hopes her face shows loyalty and determination. At the very least, she hopes it's blank.

"Well?" she asks. Too abrupt. "There was something you wanted to tell me?"

"About Brian Dexter, yes. How much do you know about him?"

"If you've read the letters, you know what I know." She can't help it if he hears resentment.

"Oh, I haven't read them, the prison guys do that." And just what sort of work is it, reading other people's letters: exciting, interesting, dull? Do they look at words, the way Jane can, and conjure lives? Are they at all ashamed of themselves and their jobs? "What I'm getting at is, do you know much about his history?"

No. Because she hasn't wanted to. Love must conquer all, or what's it for?

"Not really. We've written about the present mostly. What we're both doing. He's started working in the prison library, for instance. I suggested that. I work in a library here, you know. I thought he might like it, and it turns out he does. He says it's a kind of reward for good behavior there, working in the library." She is having trouble stopping herself from going on and on, leaving no spaces. Can she not make this man see that Brian, in his own environment, seems to be well thought of? That he has ambitions and resolutions? He is working in the *library*, for heaven's sake.

"You do know he's getting out."

"Yes."

"Has he mentioned where he wants to go?"

"Not exactly. Why?"

"Have you offered to do anything for him when he's released? Get him work or accommodation, anything like that?"

"Not really. He hasn't actually asked me for anything, either." This seems to her another sign of Brian's good character, or potentially good character: that he hasn't asked anything of her at all except for her letters, and a time and place to meet, to visit, and anyway, that was her idea. He's asked her for a few words from the free world, and that's just human and natural, isn't it?

"How did you come to write him in the first place?"

"Why are you asking these questions? I thought you wanted to tell me something, not ask things." That was good, wasn't it? She sounded tough there, didn't she, sure of herself, on top of events, no one to be pushed around.

"Yes, you're right." She knew that. "But I was interested. I know these guys get lonesome, but they have different ways of getting acquainted with people, that's all."

These guys? As if Brian is just one of many? He couldn't be more wrong. Brian is utterly individual and special and unique.

"If you must know, he ran an advertisement for a penpal in the newspaper and it caught my eye. I thought it wouldn't do any harm, and I can't see that it has. We've exchanged a few letters, that's all."

"According to the prison people, he got three answers to that ad, and you're the only one he's still writing to. Do you know why that would be?"

Because he's entranced by her, has huge hopes of her, has fallen in love with her, is terribly grateful, because of her words? It is thrilling, she could just hug this man for telling her that Brian's not writing to anyone else. He must have come to understand so much; perhaps he dreams about holding her, being with her. He must feel the heat even through paper and over such a distance. He must be, really, quite a man.

She shrugs. "Maybe he enjoys my letters? Maybe mine are more interesting than other people's?"

He has the grace to look a bit embarrassed. "Of course, I'm sorry, there's that, I'm sure. But also, you should know you're the only one who wrote who has a steady job and a decent income and her own apartment and lives on her own. You could be some good to him. Do you see what I mean?"

Indeed she does. He means she's the only lonely, vulnerable one. That isn't it at all. "I hope I've already been some good to him. Encouraging him to work in the library, discussing books, telling him about ordinary things that happen to me. Surely you can't think it's bad that somebody's been encouraging him to work and get some knowledge and be ready to have a job and not wind up back in jail?" She is irritated to hear that questioning lift at the end of her sentence. She wasn't intending to ask, she intended to tell.

"I know, you're absolutely right, that's very important, of course. My concern is that there could be something more involved. From his point of view, I mean. He may be expecting more than you've meant to offer."

There is no chance in the world of that.

"What if he comes here when he gets out, have you thought about that? It's just a few more days, and he has your address, he knows you're a kind person. Have you thought what you'd do if he turned up on your doorstep?"

She certainly has. "Do you think he will?"

"It's possible. And if you take my advice, you'll write him or phone the prison and make sure he understands he's not to show up and you can't help him or do anything for him."

How very blunt. Brutal. She raises her eyebrows. "Wouldn't that be unkind? I would have thought it'd be good for a prisoner to have help waiting for him. It must be hard to go out into nothing. Why should I mind helping him?"

"Because, Miss Smith, I don't think Brian Dexter is a man you really want to know." He sits back, regarding her as if that's all he needs to say.

Just what does he know about Brian Dexter—what, for that matter, does he know about her?—that he can decide all this on her behalf? He has no idea how familiar she already is, in her way, with Brian. The rest can only be details, little shadings in her picture.

This is no time to remember her own hesitations.

"You're really going to have to tell me why. You can't expect me just to take your word."

An impatient sigh. Policemen must get used to being unconditionally obeyed. "Miss Smith." He sets down his teacup, leans forward in the chair, looks at her intently, with his hands clasped together, arms settled just above his knees, so that they extend beyond his legs into air, into her space. "Brian Dexter is thirty-eight years old." She knows that, so what? "He's been in and out of trouble since he was a teenager." Poor Brian, then, an unhappy childhood, confused upbringing, possibly unloved, un-wanted—she can make all that up to him.

She wants to put her arms around him and tell him, "Brian, whatever happened to you, you're loved *now*. Enough to make up for anything."

"Break-and-enters when he was a kid." But that was when he was a kid and wouldn't understand, or care, about the terror of coming home to find your possessions, your home, rifled, emptied, vandalized. Kids don't own anything, they don't have their own places, so how could they know how it feels?

Jane herself has two deadbolts on her door.

"He graduated to heavier stuff in his twenties. Got convicted for a couple of armed robberies, milk stores. He threatened the clerks with a gun. Turned out it wasn't a real gun, but they didn't know that." But Brian knew it. He never meant to hurt anyone. He must have been so poor, so desperate.

It's hard, though, not to consider the clerks: how frightened they must have been, not knowing the gun was only fake. Still, the main thing is, Brian's intention was essentially harmless.

"Got a couple of years for that. Reformatory, not prison—two years less a day was the sentence, and that keeps you out of the big time. But it's rough enough, and he had some bad times inside." She can just imagine: she's seen enough movies, she knows what sorts of brutalities occur in jails. Brian's going to need more love and tenderness than even she has dreamed so far, but she is going to make it up to him. She is going to make everything better. She is grateful to this man for giving her so much to work with. How needed she will be!

"He also got connected with some hard cases. When he got out he was a drug user, and he started dealing to support himself. He also turned into a major drinker."

But he can hardly be doing those things now. He's been in prison for ten years! It must be about time to hear some of his more recent, more redemptive qualities.

"He did a few odd jobs, worked in an auto body joint for a while, that kind of thing. He was good with his hands when he was sober, but he couldn't stay that way, so he kept getting fired. He started hanging out with the sister of one of his reformatory buddies. She was just a kid, and he was twenty-six by then. He knocked—got her pregnant, so they got married."

Now Jane, sitting back abruptly, *is* appalled. Brian has a family, a wife, a child, perhaps more. Her life just went out the window.

He'd started to say Brian had knocked this girl up, and changed it to "got her pregnant," in delicate deference to Jane—a pointless daintiness, given the brutality of his other words.

"Look, Miss Smith, I don't think you want to hear all this. Would you take my word for it now that he's not somebody you want to know?" It occurs to her that all along, he's been calling her Miss Smith. How does he know it isn't Mrs.? After all, she might be divorced, or a widow. And is there something pathetic and unassertive about her that tells him she isn't Ms Smith, either?

No, she wouldn't take his word. Even if he isn't lying (and she has to admit, none of this sounds like a lie; only a heartbreak), she would never say, "All right, you can stop now." Because you don't put down a book, some tale of great romance, at the point where the lovers have quarreled, where there's been a terrible misunderstanding that's led to separation. No, you keep reading right through, knowing the sorrows will only make the reconciliation more joyful and more loving in the end.

In Jane's books, the heroes do not have wives and children. What family does this policeman have? Possibly a wife who worries, as Jane understands the spouses of police do worry, whenever he goes on duty? While he's sitting here in Jane's small pastel living room, doing an odd sort of duty, is some woman drawing pictures of him in peril?

"Do you have a family?"

She doesn't particularly care that he looks startled. To him, of course the question must sound, at best, irrelevant.

"Yes, I do," he says quietly, "but I'm not here to talk about myself." No, he's here to talk about Brian. Ruin her life. This is as beyond her control as a speeding train, or cancer cells, or any disaster, really. (And her faith in inevitability is once again confirmed.)

"Go on," she says. He sighs. He also turns his wrist slightly, glancing down, checking his gold-banded watch. Is he bored? Is all this too time-consuming? This is costing him an hour, say. There is no pricetag on what it's costing her. Or Brian.

"Okay," he resumes briskly. "His wife's name was Janet. Kind of a street kid, little and pretty tough. But young, anyway. She'd only just turned seventeen, and she was six

173

months pregnant when he got mad one night and killed her."

No. That's a lie. Jane can't be hearing right. What appetite for vengeance would cause this man to make up such a thing?

"He'd beaten her up before, and then got beat up by her brother, but this time he killed her. With his fists, Miss Smith. He bashed her head around for a while against the kitchen wall and then the floor, but what killed her was when he hit her in the stomach and she hemorrhaged. He was sentenced to eight years."

No.

"Then he had a few problems inside, so time kept getting added. We're not talking about a rocket scientist here, Miss Smith. He was caught in a couple of punch-ups, and then trying to escape. But now he's getting out legit. And I really don't think you want to know him."

Wait a minute, give her time. Given time, Jane can almost always look on the bright side.

Actually, and no doubt this is pretty terrible, but after that first disbelief, Jane's next feeling is relief: that Brian does not, after all, have a wife or a child. He is, after all, emerging into the world, to her, all alone.

She can't think about the rest of it.

"Miss Smith?" asks this Sergeant Barnes. "Are you okay?"

Does she not look okay? Well, perhaps not. Beyond her normal plainness there's too much to contain. There's violence in the swiftness of opposing feelings, the swing between lost dreams and relief. She can see violence, she can understand being simply overwhelmed.

And what about circumstances? This man seems to be omitting those, has failed to mention whatever rages and frustrations and pains led Brian to do what he apparently did. Maybe Brian found out it wasn't his child. Maybe his wife wouldn't do certain things—Sergeant Barnes said she was tough, a street kid. What does Jane know of young girls like that? They must be difficult to live with.

Poor Brian. Such a topsy-turvy life. Such a life of lovelessness and loss.

"Look," he says. "It's very nice to write letters, but there are dangers, too. It's important to know what you're doing, so you don't get in over your head."

How can he say that? He had no idea what he was doing, coming here, but he came ahead anyway, didn't he? And then he worries about her drowning, in over her head?

Poor Brian. How he must need her.

Still, a new, if somewhat dim and unfocused, picture is presenting itself: a large man looming over a small pregnant girl. Jane sees her dark-haired, skinny except for her belly.

That man isn't Jane's Brian. And if it once was, it was only for a moment. He must have been so sorry! He must have looked down afterward and wondered how he could ever have done such a thing, and regarded his fists with amazement at what they'd carried out all by themselves. He'd think, "How could that happen when I didn't want it to?" Because he would never have wanted such a thing. No one would.

And he must have mourned the baby, too. He would have been a good father. Being a father would have changed his life. He wouldn't have had to wait an extra ten years to learn about tenderness, he would have known all about it, the instant he first held his child. Poor Brian, such a waste, what a tragedy.

Although without that waste and tragedy, they would never have come together, he and Jane. This must be how life works: events can seem vicious and meaningless for years, until there's suddenly a moment when they fit together and make a sort of beautiful, benevolent, if sorrowful, sense.

She thinks of her own child: the little dark-haired chubby girl, all filled with love. How could she now leave that child with him?

How is Brian worse than this man here in her living room, who also comes into a home smashing things?

"Miss Smith, do you understand what I've been saying?" She nods, lacking words. "Then you'll do what I said? You'll make it clear to him he can't come here or count on you for anything when he gets out?"

Again she nods. If he leaves assuming he's succeeded, it doesn't matter.

"Good. Then I'll go now. I can see myself out." Standing, moving past her, he puts a hand down briefly on her shoulder. Pity is a terrible thing.

She hears the door close, but doesn't unbend. If she unbent, what might happen? Maybe she would lose herself, the way Brian must have done that night (it must have happened at night, that's when feelings and desires can be particularly odd, vivid, and dangerous).

Is it true that people wind up facing what they fear most? People terrified of traffic may die in a car crash, people horrified by loneliness may find themselves living desolately alone. People drive themselves crazy with worry over losing their minds. Jane, fearful of disorder and terror itself, may wind up with violence? This is an awfully cruel joke, if it's true, Jane would say.

It's time to go to bed, but how can she? Brian is waiting there, as he has been every night for weeks. In the darkness she has traced his bones, as he has traced hers. Their child has slept sweetly in another room; but safely?

"Tell me," she wishes she had asked Sergeant Barnes, "what does he look like? What color are his eyes and hair? Does he smile easily? Are there lines around his eyes?" Anything at all. She needs to know more than his beauty now, she needs to know configurations and relationships, how his features fit together. "Tell me what he looks like," she would ask.

Sergeant Barnes would have been astonished. He would have thought, "After all that, she wants to know what he looks like? The woman's an idiot, she deserves what she gets, she's too stupid to live."

Even so, she wants to know.

This place, her cherished apartment, feels empty—and slightly menacing. Jane could use a friend tonight.

Is it odd that when she invents characters, they are a pair of hands, or a lover, or a tiny child, never a friend? She can't picture anyone knowing as much about her as a friend would have to: her frailties and hopes. Which in some ways are identical.

If Brian needed her, he might be a friend. He has such terrible secrets himself—how could he ever be startled by hers? There are ways in which, she must say, she might be a match for Brian Dexter.

Lucy and little Lydia might know men like Brian. (It doesn't do to consider too closely the possibility that they've known at least one man perhaps very like Brian.) Jane could visit Lucy tomorrow, and they could sit on Lucy's littered sofa and do each other's hair and nails and Jane could hear all about men like Brian.

Hardly. Lucy may know some things that are a mystery to Jane, but she would never recognize a magic man.

Some women would no doubt call their mothers. But women who could call their mothers wouldn't find themselves in this sort of spot, would they? Anyway, she knows what her mother would say: something like, "Jane, you are a fool." This would be a judgment, hardly a discussion.

Marcy? She must know all kinds of men.

Not like Brian. No one knows anyone like Brian, who is unique and beautiful and has been Jane's life for weeks and months, who is invisible and possibly quite dangerous, and who is coming here in the flesh, or is not coming here if Jane decides to take steps.

Decides? Among all the other things that are so unfair right at the moment, it is surely unjust that Jane's very first decision (as opposed to circumstances she has merely drifted into) is so life-altering, and possibly life-threatening. Perhaps in twenty-eight years, she ought to have taken some decision-making baby steps, gotten some practice, made some little mistakes.

Because this way is very hard.

12

A person might reasonably wonder where on earth Jane has been for twenty-eight years. Can she really believe life has some built-in inclination toward fairness?

She isn't exactly stupid, she does read newspapers on occasion, and often catches the television news. Does she think all those people in disastrous circumstances have brought them on themselves?

Perhaps. In some silent section of her mind, she may believe exactly that. Many people do, although they wouldn't dream of saying it out loud. It would sound too cruel, whereas kept unconsidered to themselves, it just feels comforting.

Because who can feel too guilty about good fortune, if after all it's only what's deserved; and who can feel too responsible for the misfortunes of others if that also is deserved, although for reasons that are not necessarily apparent?

Jane, for instance, is as able as the rest of us to read about the hungry and homeless and put down the paper feeling merely pleased to have taken better care of herself than *that,* at least. Touched by images of famine, she writes the odd cheque to agencies that claim to feed the starving in countries far away. Is that fair, that people starve? It may be part of some grand scheme. There must be a reason, even if she can't think just what it is.

To have stayed so removed, so untouched and pristine in her second-floor apartment, watching warily when she's out but safe by and large—it makes it a good deal easier to have faith in fairness.

Now she can't be so sure. She can't assume anything at all. She is about to be touched by the hand, if not the fist, of real event.

How much simpler and clearer it's been to see herself from the outside, as if her life really were on television. From the outside there's such a comforting long view.

And really, from the inside, too. How touched has she been by Lydia and Lucy, after all? Or by Jim, or even her own mother? These people all struggle with real and disastrous events right in her presence, and she manages to retain, even grips more firmly, her own dispassion.

See? She's doing it again, she has managed to shift back even from her own life, just in these last few moments.

This may be a luxury she isn't going to have much longer. All sorts of things are going to change, one way or another, and this could be among the first.

It's hard to sit still, hard to keep her mind from leaping from this to that; hard also to feel entirely secure and untouchable within the sanctuary of this apartment.

She needs to get outside this place, the scene of her future now faintly chilling.

It's late, hours and hours since darkness. At least, though, she might go downstairs?

A step, anyway.

And doesn't Jim owe her a crisis? She may owe him a confession and a secret. Is this the perfect confluence of friendship?

Since his bad night, it's been quiet downstairs: no parties, no raised voices, no laughter, no music. What is he doing down there? She remembers thinking he could be her friend, and feeling tenderly toward him, but what sort of friend has she been? She hasn't even knocked on his door to see if he's still alive. Talk about detachment! Or, as her father might say, easy come, easy go—sensations, desires, even pity and concern, skittering along Jane's surface and away, like water striders.

She doesn't knock very loudly, in case he's asleep. She hears footsteps, and when he opens the door, his "Hello, Jane" sounds surprised. Is he more gaunt than before? His hair is drifting down across his forehead and sticking up at the back. His eyes are unclear. Perhaps he was napping, if not actually in bed. Sometimes, watching television at night, Jane drifts off, too. "Is something the matter?"

It occurs even to Jane, just for an instant, that there's something not very nice when somebody assumes there's something wrong just because a person knocks at a door. What does it say about her, that she wouldn't otherwise appear?

"I was thinking about you. Wondering." Unprepared, she never expresses herself very well. It's unlike her to have simply come down the stairs and knocked, unprepared.

Who knows what's like or unlike her any more? Even she can no longer make these assumptions.

"Could I come in? Unless you're busy. Am I interrupting something?" Because who knows how his life may have restored itself, who knows what he's up to now?

"Sure." He opens the door wider, stepping back and ushering her in with a wave of his hand.

Goodness! Except that the layout of the rooms here mirrors her place, she is in a different world entirely. She had imagined something quite similar to her own:

feminine, light-colored, soft-textured, tasteful; perhaps with more odds and ends, bits of art of one kind and another, but recognizable as originating in a culture similar to hers.

Instead she has stepped into a universe of maleness: leather furniture, rough dark brown carpet with a slight blue weave, deep maroon club chairs and green-shaded lamps, and over in the corner a solid, heavy desk with papers scattered over it. There is no *lightness* to the place: as if Jim and Steve were afraid that otherwise they might fly right up and out of it.

Jane can see, looking around, the appeal of all this.

There is a smell, also, of something male: pipe tobacco, aftershave? Not flowers or candles.

"Great place," she says, sinking into leather. The material beneath her is incredibly smooth, soft. Whatever made her think that flowered cushions on wicker were so comfortable?

She would not in a million years be able to afford leather. She also knows the sort of pricetags carried by a rug like this, and those green-shaded executive lamps. What exactly does Jim (and did Steve) do for a living? Are they rich, or is this just where all their money's gone?

Also, is this the sort of atmosphere Brian would prefer? Perhaps not. Perhaps he wouldn't require this extremism, which has no softening touch that she can see. Brian, so male, might not need to point it out with such an emphatic hand.

"This is nice," he says. "I'm glad you dropped down. I was just feeling sorry for myself and lonesome, and here you are!"

Imagine being able to say something like that. Imagine her saying to anyone who dropped by, "I was just feeling sorry for myself and lonesome."

Nice to be regarded as a piece of good fortune.

He's hardly a man lacking shrewdness, however. He's no fool. "Is anything wrong?"

"I don't know." And really, she doesn't. For all she knows, all may be right. "I felt like talking to somebody, though, and I thought maybe you wouldn't mind." Even this much feels like a revelation, and brave.

"Of course I don't mind. This is nice. I'll get you a drink. Wine okay?" He seems cheered by her need, which isn't very nice, really. But "Listen," he says, sitting beside her, shifting himself slightly sideways so that he's half-facing her (and she turns to half-face him), "I should have thanked you before for saving my life the other night. I really appreciate it. I wish we'd gotten to know each other before. Why didn't we?" He doesn't leave her time to answer, if she had an acceptable answer. "We thought," he laughs, "you didn't like gay men. Or gay anything. Because you wouldn't come to our parties."

"I didn't think I'd fit in very well." She might have found a better way to put that. "I thought you were nice to ask me, though. I always thought you were probably nice."

Just as Brian thinks she's nice. There seems to be a lot of niceness around, and where does that get anybody?

Show an interest in a friend, Jane. "How are you getting along?"

"Without Steve? Not very well." He looks sad—perhaps she shouldn't have asked. "I guess it just takes time. That's what people say, anyway. I didn't understand how quiet the place could get. Even if he wasn't listening, I could always talk to him. I even miss the sound of my own voice, never mind his. But I suppose they're right, I'll get used to it. People keep saying I should get out and they keep asking me places, but I haven't felt like it yet. Do you really not find it hard living alone?"

Yes, as a matter of fact. "I don't know. I always have, since I left home. Mainly it's okay. I mean, it's nice to come home to a quiet place after being with people all day, and you don't always have to be thinking about what another person's doing or what they think of what you're doing. It's okay." She shrugs. And it's true that right now it really doesn't seem so terrible. "The trouble is, I don't know if it's going to stay that way. Everything may change really soon. That's why I came down, to see if you had time to give me some advice."

His down-drawn face lights up. "Oh, isn't that lovely. Are we such friends, then?"

Somewhat excessive, a bit overstated for Jane's tastes. She shrinks back, but then again, he is precisely right: they may be (in a way) friends, and it could be lovely. "I guess so," she says.

"I think it's wonderful you want to tell me, and also, if you don't mind my saying so, it'll give me a chance to start paying you back for saving my life." That's twice he's said that. Does he mean that if she hadn't called him upstairs that night and listened to him, he'd have killed himself? Not likely. It's just his way of speaking, an exaggeratedness that could, if she got used to it, become appealing.

He has also said what she thought earlier: that he owes her, and that he can now pay her back. Friends.

Only, how do friends talk to each other? How truthful are they likely to be?

"Probably," she warns him, and herself, "you're going to think I'm crazy. I haven't told a soul yet, but now I have to do something."

"I won't think you're crazy. I promise." He pats her hand. She supposes that will have to do by way of reassurance.

184

So starting with the advertisement and her first letter, she launches briskly into her tale, telling its main points with surprisingly little stumbling. Also surprisingly, it doesn't take long; likely because she leaves out just about everything important, telling only facts, and even fudging some of those. "I just thought it might help him, to have someone to write to. And now this!"

"But you invited him to come here?" Jim may not think she's crazy, but he does sound astonished. As well he might be. As she is.

"Well yes, but I didn't see the harm. I'm not sure I see any now. It's only, that policeman, he was so serious. I don't know. What should I do?"

"What do you want to do?"

She wants to run away, even if it means leaving behind all those new clothes, the wallpapering and decorating and the fresh flowers and the candles, her books and her TV, her bed, her whole life. She also wants the life she has seen so clearly. "I don't know. I never expected this."

Well, she did though, didn't she? She expected precisely that Brian would come. She just never gave him a story of his own; and she never dreamed of ambivalence.

"Aren't you scared of him? I would be."

"I don't know." She doesn't seem to know much at all.

"The cop didn't tell you what kind of guy he is now?"

"Not really. Just what happened, I guess. I don't think he knows him, he only came because it was sort of an errand. I think the prison people suggested it."

"But that must tell you something, right?"

"Except I don't know what. Somebody might just want to hurt him, or keep him from improving himself or something." This does sound feeble. Why would they go to so much trouble just to make one man's life (and as a side-effect hers) more difficult? "It's really hard to know."

"You believe he did what the cop said, though."

"I guess I have to. I mean, it's the kind of thing I could check, so it has to be true."

"What kind of guy does he sound like from his letters?"

The trouble is, she can't properly describe the words she's heard between the lines, so what is left? "Not very educated, but trying to improve himself. He says he's changed, that he used to be wild but doesn't want to be any more. He wants to settle down. I don't know."

"The cop said he beat his wife? With his fists?"

"That's what he said."

"Jesus."

"Well yes. Only Brian says he's changed."

"But he's never told you what he did?"

"No, but then, I never asked."

"Why not?"

Why indeed. Because she didn't want to know. Because she has no gift for facts, and not much inclination toward truth. "I thought he'd tell me in his own time. Or that it didn't matter." How stupid that sounds, said aloud.

Suddenly he grins. "Rough trade, Jane. You're into some very rough trade."

Is that some kind of joke? What does that mean, rough trade? Well, she can guess. And it isn't very nice. This isn't him and his friends laughing in a bar, this is her *life*. Perhaps literally it's her life. How can she know? A friend would take it seriously.

"I'm sorry, Jane. You have to admit, though, it's got its funny side."

She has to admit no such thing.

"It's late." She stands. "I should go. Thanks for listening." This is why there's little point in having friends, after all: it appears they're likely to be as little involved in her concerns as she has been in theirs.

(How easy it seems to be, this shift from shyness to cynicism.)

"What will you do, though? We haven't decided what you should do." He reaches for her hand, to pull her back down.

"I know, but after all, it's not the kind of thing I can really ask somebody else to decide. I'll have to, that's all. But it did help, that you listened." This, she realizes, having said it only from politeness, is true. To put the thing into words has been kind of a shock, if only that starting-to-become-familiar shock of real event; but it has also given it context and perspective, taking it slightly away from herself. Like seeing her apartment from the point of view of someone who hasn't been there before. Maybe that's the kind of thing friends do, even if they can't actually solve or really protect. She is still a little offended, but anyway, says, "Thanks, Jim."

"Nothing to it. Let me know what I can do. I can phone the prison for you, if you want. Or I can wait for him with you. Whatever." Standing at the door to let her out, he leans down, the way he did at her place before, only this time kisses her lightly on the forehead instead of putting his arms around her. This is nice, too. "Now tell me, are you scared? Worried?"

"Not right now." Mostly now, she's tired.

"And you're okay on your own? You're welcome to stay, you know."

"I'll be fine, really."

"Well if you're not, you come back. No problem, no matter what time it is. Just bang on the door."

"Thank you." She really means it, too. Look what she's been missing, him living right below her all this time.

But before, he had his own life and never needed her either.

How do people come to conclusions, anyway?

Well, Brian's young wife found a way, didn't she? She let him come to a conclusion for her.

Jane lets herself back into her apartment, gets ready for bed, climbs under the duvet, switches off the bedside light. Finds herself staring up into darkness.

What the hell is she going to do?

Nothing is solved, talking it over.

It feels as if Brian knows a good deal more about her than she knows about him. That can hardly be true, though, can it, given what she now knows about him? But what if a guard, or a warden, or whatever they have in that place, told Brian that his past would be revealed to her. So he wrote his last letter with a view to making himself sound harmless and hopeful and cured.

It's been such a blessing going to bed the past few months. What wonderful things have occurred! Now she can imagine becoming afraid to go to bed, for fear of the night. If she lets Brian come, she may need to stay alert; and even if she doesn't, she may hear his footsteps anyway.

Still, perhaps her only flaw is this fear, these images that flash like photographs, brushing past quickly, because how could she really look at them? If she could cure fear, that would solve everything. Because has she not intended perfect companionship, perfect affection? There can't be any fault in her except fear, not the way there may have been in a pregnant teenaged girl, a street kid, tough and perhaps unwise.

How Jane longs for her own Brian Dexter, though: her sweet, warm, strong, tender, and protective Brian. She can see Sergeant Barnes washing his hands, quite literally, when he got back to work. Very likely he hasn't spared her another thought since, and if he has, it would only be to hope vaguely that she truly has been persuaded. But anyway, he would think, it's up to her now.

There will have to be even more secrets than she'd intended. She won't ever be able to tell Marcy, or her mother, or anyone else (besides Jim, and that may have been a mistake) that Brian killed his wife. She might go so far as to say, "Oh, he robbed a couple of stores," which is apparently true. Now that seems such a *mild* activity. "But he's gone straight," she could add. "He has a good job, and he's settled down, and really, in a way it's probably good those things happened when he was young. He appreciates everything now, he knows how great it is. Most people don't, you know. They have nothing to compare their lives to. Brian, though, he's been around, he's done it all." And having done it all, has decided she is his best possibility—a very great compliment.

She certainly can't tell anyone the worst. "It turns out," she would have to say, "he murdered his wife. He beat her to death. That wasn't the first thing he'd done, either. He says he's different now, and it's true he is older, but how can I know? How could I ever sleep? He'll be here very soon."

Marcy, say, would throw up her hands. "Good grief, Jane, I don't know what you should do. Whatever possessed you? Didn't you *think?*"

Well no, she didn't. But she certainly felt, and hoped.

And, it must be said, still does.

Let him know, he writes, if she's changed her mind and no longer wants him to come. He'll understand, he says. She could do that, she could write (because it would be hard actually to hear his voice, and possibly dangerous, if she used just the wrong tone herself) and say, "No, don't come. I've learned some things you didn't tell me (and I didn't ask), and I don't want you here any more. You're far too real for me." If she did that, would she be able to sleep? Without nightmares?

Then what hope could she ever have again? She would have before her forty, fifty, sixty years of nights without nightmares. Also nights without arms. There is terror in every direction.

What will her mother say?

Even without knowing the whole truth, it may take her mind, at least briefly, off her own troubles. She may pause from wondering how she will die to wonder how her daughter will live. She may be curious enough about Brian, or worried enough, to forget her own encroaching, mysterious pain.

Or she may be happy enough to see her daughter settled. She might even be glad for Jane. She might see all this as romantic and exciting. She might think of Brian as glamorous or compelling. She could be quite taken with him, really.

She will have to be interested, at least. This may be the first time Jane has been able to capture her interest. She might look at Jane and say mildly, "What a very peculiar thing to do, dear. I'd never have thought it of you. But good luck, of course. I wish you the best." Then, more practically, she might add, "I'll be leaving you the house and some insurance and some other odds and ends. You never know when you'll need money of your own." Jane remembers that her mother, so businesslike beneath the gloss, was grateful, when Jane's father died, for the house and his insurance. Probably, however disgusted Jane was at the time, this made sense. And it makes sense that what belonged to her father should not wind up in Brian's hands.

Those hands!

What would her father think of all this? He might be furious with her for getting herself into this spot, or with Brian for—what, taking advantage of her? Is that what he's done? Or he might be pleased to have her taken care of, one way or another, at least safer than she is on her own. Unlike her mother, he might have spotted on Jane's face the exhaustion of always being responsible, never getting a break from herself.

She has no idea what he would think. That's a bit sad.

Finally, she sleeps. But when she does, fists come at her in her dreams. There are menacing, if handsome faces, and she has no doubt when she wakes up with the sun that all of them were him.

She must have slept very restlessly; the duvet is heaped on the floor. Certainly she doesn't feel rested, and can barely pull herself out of bed. The day stretches ahead like a series of hurdles. It seems impossible to do her exercises (although she does—there's no telling yet if there's a point to having this perfect body) and difficult, also, to make her way to work and up those steps and through the doors, and to her desk. To be able to nod at people and smile as if there's nothing at all on her mind except saying hello and doing her work.

Still, there's a lot to be said for having work to do, and particular expressions to wear and words to say. Something to comfort and to hide behind. She can carry this off.

191

And look what other people must have to carry off, every day. Marcy, say: concerns about Simone, about a shattered marriage, about making a living, about triggering a union drive, about, no doubt, romance. And is it ever possible to hear any of that in her voice? True, her heart isn't in her work, apparently, but Jane is beginning to see that the heart isn't always necessary. Just the functions are often sufficient. These days, too, there are the smiles and small furtive waves of people conspiring. Some sorts of secrets, Jane thinks, settling down to type, are a good way to bring people together.

But who will look after her if trouble results?

Just before lunch, Marcy slips into Jane's office, leans over Jane's desk and smiles. "We've done it," she whispers.

"What?"

"Got enough signatures. We're a union, and there's nothing anybody can do about it."

Oh, triumph! It no longer feels like a huge triumph, or even an important one in view of all Jane's other events, but still she grins back at Marcy.

"We're having another meeting Thursday night to elect an executive, all that. Can you come?"

Of course Jane can come. Anyway, she has to, now that she's not only in so deep but on the winning side. "Sure. How about my place this time?" She'd like these people to see where she lives, to admire her taste. Then when Brian comes, they'll be able to picture him and Jane together there.

Oh heavens.

"I'd rather mine again, if that's okay. Otherwise it's hard, because I can't leave Simone." Well, she leaves her on other evenings, for other occasions, doesn't she?

On the other hand: Simone. Jane is dazzled by what Simone must mean to Marcy.

Jane could take Simone a small gift. What do four-year-olds like? Perhaps a small stuffed toy. Or a book—it appears that Simone enjoys books.

What would Jane and Brian's child enjoy? Books, for sure. Music. Embraces. Their child would enjoy most of all sitting in her lap, being cradled and rocked. Their child would enjoy being loved.

What if their child reminded Brian of the one he doesn't have? There are a great many things, it seems, that people can't bear.

Jane herself can't bear other people's voices. What she can imagine they'll say. What if her life became an entertainment? What if people at work went around saying to each other, "Did you hear about Jane? Poor thing, can you believe it, she's been writing letters to this horrible prisoner and now that he's getting out, she has this idea he'll move in with her and they'll live happily ever after. Even have kids. Can you imagine anything more pathetic?" Or, "Did you hear about Jane? Poor thing, she's been writing letters to this horrible prisoner and now he's getting out and she's absolutely terrified he's going to land on her doorstep. Except she asked him to. Can you imagine anything so stupid?"

She could tell this sort of thing to Brian. Her Brian, she means, not the nightmare one with the terrible fists. She wants to write him again, right away. She has so much news and so many questions, she could write him every day, every free hour, more than a letter a day. She badly needs to know her Brian's there, listening and reading.

And what would he think of such an avalanche? He probably wouldn't be allowed to get it all anyway, there are likely restrictions on the letters he gets, as well as the ones he sends.

Then there are those faceless prison readers, would they feel it necessary to call Sergeant Barnes? Say something like, "What the hell did you say to her? She's turned on like a tap, she's writing like crazy."

Brian might think something like that, also. He might make jokes with his cellmates, or pass her correspondence around the library. Rude words might be said, filthy gestures made, there might be nasty jokes about his future.

Not *her* Brian. He'd never allow anything like that. Her Brian keeps her in his possession as a secret, like a pearl. Any violence in his heart, well, he'd use it to protect her.

On her way home she stops at a drugstore for magazines. Surely in one of them there will be a new way to get her hair cut that will make some huge and crucial difference. There's one that promises whole makeovers: page after page of before-and-after pictures, the befores perfect shambles of womanhood, the afters perfect women.

These hints and clues are important for the moment of opening the door. It will be that first impression that is vital: what he first sees.

What will she see?

Also she stops at a department store to buy more rolls of yarn, this time a deep, rich blue, almost a sea-blue-green. If she works at it, she can get the beige sweater finished and a second one under way in just the next few days. Won't they demonstrate his welcome, her warmth, their safety together?

Or they could still be gifts, but somewhat pleading, mitigating ones. She could send them, by quickest mail possible, to the prison, telling him, "I care, see how much I care? But please leave me alone, after all. These sweaters, really, are the best I can do for you. Do you understand? Please understand."

Is Brian a man who listens to pleading?

His wife, she must have pleaded, and it seems he didn't care. Apparently it didn't slow him down for a moment.

But as he says, he's changed. So has Jane. In just these few months she's taken a number of tiny new steps, and that's nothing like a whole ten years, so who knows how either of them—both of them—might wind up? Obviously, anything is possible. There are ways to see that as encouraging, and Jane is trying very hard.

13

So little time, so much to do.

This does not include writing Brian, despite those impulses to confide. Whatever Jane would like to tell him, or ask him, what he wants to hear is whether or not he is welcome; she can hardly write and leave the matter unaddressed. "Yes, come," or "No, please don't," is all he's looking for, and she can't write either one.

So here she is on her own, as lonely in her indecision as she's ever been.

What a comfort, then, to have so much to do—on top, of course, of her ordinary day-to-day life.

It's amazing to her, in fact, that any ordinary day-to-day life can even continue. She hears the tension of extraordinary events humming like wires overhead, but everyone else is apparently deaf.

Oh, Jane is flying, she is rolling, she can hardly bear to rest. Resting, she finds, leaves too much space for images and thoughts and an acidic kind of fretfulness. The important thing is to keep moving.

So she doesn't mind at all leaving her desk to help reshelve books. She has no objections to working while

Marcy leans on a book cart chatting with some excitement about their union triumph. It makes Jane feel like a conspirator, and even a ringleader, a view of herself that may be inaccurate but makes her feel strong and important, nevertheless.

She might consult Marcy about getting her hair done. And what should she do with her face? Marcy may have some ideas.

Really, she's feeling quite fond of Marcy. She might ask her and Simone over for tea. She might tell Marcy the story of Jim and Steve, making it amusing, in a light and brittle tone.

Well no. It can't be right to turn one friend into an amusement for another. Even inexperienced Jane can see, if not the evils, at least the perils of that.

Still, telling stories may take the sting from them. With that theory, she might also mention that her mother believes she is dying. "She's being very brave about it," Jane might say. "But we've never been close. I haven't been able to figure out what to say to her."

That would be honest enough, not really disloyal.

What lighthearted words could she say about Brian?

Mrs. Curtis stops by Jane's desk this afternoon, and pulls up a chair. "We need to have a talk, Jane," in a tone that would sound ominous to anyone listening, which Jane isn't, really.

"Oh yes?"

"Yes." How crisp! "From now on, we've decided the brochure you do every month should be double-checked before you send it out. So make sure it comes to me before it's printed, all right?"

Jane's work has included the monthly pamphlet listing upcoming events, and in her head-down, thorough way, she has done, in her view, a pretty good job, taking extra care to come up with colorful words to make events sound interesting and scavenging drawings from reference books to use as illustrations. It's a long time since it was checked by someone else. Now Mrs. Curtis is making it plain that her efforts mean nothing: that she is merely a hired hand.

It must be because of the union. Which must prove how badly a union is needed, and what authoritarian ill-will lurks beneath normal civility.

What's interesting, though, is how unmoved Jane is. She can recall a time not long ago when she would have been shattered, or at least badly wounded. Today's Jane, with far larger fish to fry in her life, merely shrugs. "Okay. We can see how that works. If it doesn't, well, it was never in my job description anyway. You could take over the whole thing."

Mrs. Curtis gasps a little, but she also stands and goes away. Jane finds that vaguely interesting, too: the power of not particularly caring.

What other uses might it have?

Tonight there's the union meeting at Marcy's. This time Jane takes along a far cheaper wine. She joins the others to elect Marcy president and head of the bargaining committee, although wondering where Marcy will find the time, and whether it's fair to Simone. If Jane had a child, she thinks, she wouldn't be wasting her time on matters that are frivolous in comparison.

"I'd like to nominate Jane for vice-president," she hears Marcy say. "I haven't mentioned this to her, but I think she'd be terrific. She has such a calm way of dealing with things, and they respect her." Others nod. The startled Jane looks like a shoo-in.

What a thrilling and surprising moment this should be! So much approval from these people she has wanted so often and so urgently to notice her.

And what considerable activity this would bring to her life: no end of meetings, gatherings, chats, after-work drinks, consultations, conspiracies, and plans. What a very full life is being offered here.

But like Marcy, Jane also has (may have) other claims on her time. Unlike Marcy, she has a keen understanding of their importance: first things first, her father would say.

"Oh, I'm afraid I couldn't." How can she explain? "I mean, I'd be happy to help out sort of unofficially, but I don't want to be tied down. I wouldn't really have enough time, so it wouldn't be fair."

Somewhat mysterious—do people's eyebrows lift? She does feel reverberations from her own words, "I don't want to be tied down," and another context: a muscular form pinning her down. To a bed, a floor, what?

Simone wanders into the room, rubbing her eyes. "I can't sleep," she complains. "You're too loud." There is, after all, a trace of a whine in the small voice. But she's tired, poor thing. Jane wonders how Brian would respond to that tone; or how she would, herself. She hopes she would want to hold the child, and rock her to sleep, maybe sing something to her. These must be activities she has read about, or seen in movies. She can't, herself, recall being rocked or sung to at bedtime. But she also can't recall whining.

If her parents were keeping her awake with guests when she was a four-year-old, she wouldn't have dared to complain. There was discipline there, some idea of who was in charge. By and large, she approves of that system. She, as a mother, would be firm.

As a mother she might have to be firm to prevent Brian from getting annoyed. He may be easily annoyed and quick to act.

Oh no, stop it, keep busy, keep occupied; because he's right at the periphery of her vision, waiting for a space to fill. Is it too melodramatic to be reminded, at jolting moments, that she may have a killer on her hands one of these days?

Maybe this weekend Marcy and Simone could come over, a small girls-together gathering with Lydia on Saturday afternoon. Or maybe Jim could come upstairs, too, so all Jane's friends could meet each other. Perhaps Jane, performing an imitation of her mother, could persuade Lydia to behave. The children might play charmingly, despite their difference in age. Jane's small apartment would feel quite full, with people and activity. The silence of her home would be broken. The sounds might be stored for the future. She might feel surrounded, and even protected.

A fanciful thought. Or a desperate one. But Jane is grasping at anything, and who would not?

After the meeting she lingers behind to ask Marcy. "Gee, that sounds like fun," Marcy says. "I didn't know you were a big sister, that's really nice. But this weekend's out, I'm sorry. We're spending it with my parents. It's my mother's birthday, and anyway, they haven't seen Simone for a while. So we'll be out of town. Some other Saturday, maybe, okay?"

"Sure." But what other Saturday? Jane's future Saturdays may all be radically altered. Remember that picture of her in T-shirt and tight, tantalizing new jeans, cleaning the kitchen floor and being reached for, hands approaching her tempting and delicious hips? Jane remembers.

The nights are getting chillier. She pulls her coat tighter and steps home quickly.

Lydia can come over anyway on Saturday, and maybe Jim, too, although it might not be a good idea for Lydia to know where she lives; who knows at what odd moments the child might start to show up on her doorstep? (But why would she, with the small interest she takes in Jane?) And Jim, it might not be wise for him, either, to get the idea he's welcome any time. What if he began popping upstairs and Brian objected? What if Brian can't stand gay men, or just can't stand Jim? What might he do?

Of course Brian may not be coming at all. He might change his mind. She has plenty of time to let him know he has to stay away. There are days yet.

Just days!

And *has* to stay away? She appears to presume he would obey.

She wishes there were a way to look into his face and see for herself, without him seeing her. Like in the movies, a line-up where witnesses to a crime peer through one-way glass at men who might be guilty, or might not. But if she could just see his face, see if his eyes are kind or angry or (most dangerously) blank, and if his lips curl up, and if there are laughter lines around his eyes and mouth, or frown lines on his forehead. It would make a big difference to know if his hair is clean or lank and dirty. Her favorite things have been tracing lines of kindness and touching hands to hair. If she could see these things, she'd know if he is her Brian.

She only has a few days! For twenty-eight years she has pretty successfully avoided a whole world of catastrophes, holocausts, brutalities everywhere and even on her doorstep. And now every moment draws her toward an edge, moving her unstoppably to a place she can't foresee.

She could protect herself, though, take steps of her own, if she decided.

Not yet.

She is getting her hair done after work, the day after the union meeting. Every event these days, from the meeting to this appointment, seems to be an occasion for revealing new aspects of herself. So much comes as a surprise!

She's done her research, clipping pictures of a range of styles: nothing extreme or bizarre, all medium-length, mainly flowing down and floating forward, all shining and radiantly healthy.

If she is shining and radiantly healthy, that may be enough to get them past that lumpy moment when she first opens the door. If she does.

It takes almost three hours to get her hair done. An hour of that is spent waiting to be looked after—worse than a doctor's office. Who could blame Jane for thinking that if she were beautiful, if she were *valued*, she would have been taken care of promptly?

"I thought maybe something like one of these," she says, handing her clutch of clippings to the young woman who finally comes. "Whatever you do, though, I need to be able to look after it myself. I don't want something fancy I can't deal with. But something smart."

Who can blame the woman for sighing? Perhaps she also rolls her eyes.

Nevertheless, whatever sort of ordeal this is for Jane, and she does have to bite her tongue (how testy she's feeling these days, in her own defense), the results, she must admit, really aren't bad. Layered and pulled for-ward, her hair now surrounds her face like a frame. "It softens your look, I think," the young woman says. Jane agrees. What it really does, she sees, is drift onto her cheeks so there's simply less face to be seen. So less plainness visible. All to the good.

"Thank you. Very nice." Despite the wait and the discomfort, Jane leaves a hefty tip.

Preparations for important events are not inexpensive.

At a drugstore on the way home, she buys a curling iron the woman at the salon recommended. "You shouldn't have any trouble styling it yourself with that," she said. Well, Jane will find out. At least there's time to practice.

More difficult, though, is the cosmetic salon. She has wondered about these places: how magic are they? Until now she has lacked the courage, or the desperation. Now she will try anything.

She has in her mind the remembrance of lies written down, and the moment that may lie ahead at her door.

So the coupon that arrives in her mailbox (that site of vital alterations), claiming to guarantee a new and glamorous appearance at a severely reduced, affordable rate, looks like potential salvation. Perhaps she should have tried this long ago, if she was so concerned about appearance.

She imagines emerging truly transformed.

How much is she willing to endure? Because this is truly an ordeal. Humiliating, these women (chic, worldly, *very* young) fussing and glossing over Jane's very own familiar if not-loved face, and at the end standing back, regarding the results of their labors on *her* body, *her* self, saying to her (and to each other), "Now, isn't that lovely? You look *so* much better, isn't it amazing what just a little effort will do?" As if they've taken some shabby old piece of furniture and restored it to a state of shining, solid value. The terrible condescension!

Also terrible, being stared at for the hours it's taken, all that close and intimate scrutiny. No plain person likes to be stared at, does she?

And what do they mean, "just a little effort"? It's taken hours and the skills of several specialists, from makeup to manicure. And to tell the truth, instead of emerging transformed, she feels ridiculous: all shaded and high-lighted, strokes of lightness and darkness splashed across her features. She hopes she doesn't run into anyone who knows her on her way home. Despite the makeup she feels naked: those longings of hers exposed, however cleverly her features have been camouflaged.

How many hours and how much concentration it would take, maintaining so much camouflage! Nothing simple about it, not like soldiers splashing dirt on their faces to move more easily in darkness. This would have to carry her through the light, an entirely different sort of exercise, and after all, her features are still her features underneath.

Even so she has added a good many cosmetics, the very ones those young women used, to her credit card. She has left carrying quite a large plastic bag containing a small smorgasbord of masks, foundations, blushers, mascaras, eyeshadows: colors intended to emphasize, others de-signed to conceal.

Her credit card bill grows and grows. What will the women in that office think this time, as Jane's receipts roll in? More than $250 at the cosmetic salon, another $60 to the hairdresser. "That Jane Smith," they may say, "look what she's doing now, and she already got all those clothes. She must be making herself over completely!"

So she is, maybe.

Now she must practice. Like a painter she will have to sit at her mirror and do herself, again and again, until she gets it right. Or comes close.

Walking home, catching glimpses of herself reflected from windows, she is startled by her unfamiliarity. Back in her apartment, she peers into the bathroom mirror. In this light, at least, she can make out her own features beneath.

Is this worth it?

It depends, she supposes. Everything at the moment depends.

She's kept herself as occupied as she can, working and fitting in these projects, but even so, at night her mind races so fast it seems her body could run miles on this energy. There is no rest, not even when she sleeps, because then the pictures are not only terrible but out of control, and she wakes exhausted. She can remember when nightmares went away when she woke up, getting foggy and unclear until they vanished except for little leftover shivers. Now they pile up, repeating themselves until they're so real and vivid they're unforgettable. But she certainly doesn't want to think about them. She has no intention of describing them, even to herself.

Anyway, nightmares are only fear, no reflection on reality. She thinks it's maybe even good to get them out of her system beforehand.

Before something she hasn't managed to decide yet.

There are more things to be done, taken care of, wrapped up.

"I thought," she tells Lydia when she picks her up Saturday afternoon, "we'd go to my place today. You haven't been there before, and I thought it'd be nice if we had lunch there."

"Just us?"

"Yes. Although I might ask the downstairs tenant if he's around. He's a nice man."

"I'd rather you didn't," says Lucy, looking worried. This is something Jane hadn't thought of: that Lucy might have fears that Jane—Jane!—has some terrible designs on her child. Or would expose her to the designs of someone else. That's something, isn't it, to have someone worried about her potential for decadence; almost a compliment, in a funny way.

"Don't worry," Jane tells her. "He's gay."

Apparently Lucy doesn't find this reassuring. "No, really, if you're going to take her to your place, I'd just as soon it was only the two of you."

"Okay. He's harmless, but that's fine. You know, Lucy, you could come too. Do you want to? I have plenty of food." Let's just see how concerned she is.

"Thanks, but I can't. I've got company coming and then we're going to a sale." Oh well, a sale: no mother could be expected to give that up to guarantee her daughter's safety, could she? Jane almost smiles. She could almost be angry. This is exactly the sort of negligence that must have permitted so much damage to Lydia in the first place. Does the child not realize that? How can she not hate a woman who is so careless about her?

Jane's child will be very closely guarded. Damage and pain will not be permissible.

Damage and pain at whose hands? Guarded against whom? "Okay, let's get a move on, Lydia. We've got some cooking to do."

Jane has plans for the day, matters that must be dealt with.

First the two of them will work together chopping vegetables for salad, peeling hard-cooked eggs for egg salad sandwiches, mixing muffins. Mainly this will be a lesson for Lydia, but Jane also realizes she doesn't know much herself about the rituals of food, and should get better acquainted with them. It will be important to impress Brian, even more than Lydia, to stimulate a respect or admiration that might make him hesitate.

Hesitate to what?

"Is this your house?" Lydia asks with gratifying wonder, when they arrive at Jane's.

"I don't own it, no. I have the apartment upstairs." To Lydia, this will be amazing enough.

Upstairs, Lydia stands just inside the door for a moment, looking around. "Wow. This is great!" This is information she can take home with her: here's what can be done.

Jane hasn't taken Lydia's curiosity and restlessness into account. How irritating, to have this child roaming Jane's rooms, picking up this and that—vases, books, small pieces of pottery—and setting them down someplace else entirely. "Be careful, those things are breakable," Jane warns. Though Lydia does seem to be careful; at least nothing gets broken, only shifted out of place.

"Everything's so *pretty*," Lydia breathes. "It must cost an awful lot."

"Not so much. I just do things a little at a time. Please don't bounce on the furniture, okay? Come on, let's get lunch."

But Lydia keeps wandering off. "Please don't play with the TV. Look, do you want to stir the raisins into the muffin mix?"

Actually, Lydia does seem to enjoy that, although she makes a mess on the counter and comes close to burning herself on the oven door putting the muffins in. "Do you bake all the time?"

Joan Barfoot

"Pretty often." Not true, but it will be. "Things you make yourself taste better, I think. And it isn't as expensive as buying them already made." Oh, she is sending Lydia home filled with new ideas! "Tell you what, let me give you the recipe book I used for these. It's got all sorts of good stuff in it. You and your mother might like using it."

Lydia likes the egg salad, too. "That's because when you make it yourself, you can put in good things like onions and spices," Jane explains.

"Did you make this place yourself?"

"You mean the painting and wallpapering, all that? Oh yes. You can find really nice wallpaper at discount stores, you know, and it's not so hard to put on if you practice for a while. It's fun to make a room look nice."

"Could I do it?"

"Well," Jane regards her dubiously, "you might be a little too short to reach as high as you need to. But I'm sure you could help your mother, if she wanted to try."

For the first time, Jane sees something finally dawning in Lydia.

Into the cookbook she tucks a slip of paper on which she has written the name, address, and phone number of a cheap wallpaper store. "Here, you can take all this home with you. Ask your mother if she's interested."

So: one task taken care of. The harder one ahead.

"Sit down, Lydia," she says, pulling the child down beside her on the loveseat. "I want to ask you something."

"Okay." How guileless Lydia looks. But then, why wouldn't she?

"Have you ever thought," Jane asks carefully, "whether you might like another kind of big sister?"

"What?"

"You should say 'I beg your pardon,' not 'what'," Jane corrects automatically. "I mean, wouldn't you rather have one you could have more fun with? It's just, you and I don't always enjoy the same things, and I think sometimes you must find me kind of dull."

"What?" Lydia repeats. Is she stupid? Certainly she's making this more difficult than it needs to be.

"Well, look, I don't like *playing* as much as you do. I was thinking, what if you got somebody who'd do things like take you bowling or skating, stuff like that?"

"We could do that."

"Yes, I suppose. Anyway, I was just thinking you might rather have a big sister you'd have more in common with."

There's quite a silence before Lydia looks up—blankly? bleakly?—at Jane. "Don't you want me any more?"

Well, no. Or it may not be possible any more. Except put into words the way Lydia has done, it sounds intolerably cruel. And of course *is* intolerably cruel. Poor kid, that isn't what Jane meant. At least she never meant to hurt her feelings.

If Jane has never been able to quite comprehend Lydia's history, she certainly knows this kind of pain. She finds herself moving closer and putting her arm around Lydia. "Of course I want you, that wasn't what I meant. I only thought you could likely do better. Find somebody to have more fun with."

"Okay." Lydia's narrow shoulders shrug.

That's it? After all that? "It's not that I don't want to be your big sister," Jane goes on rather desperately, "I only want what's best for you."

"Sure. Yeah. Somebody else might be fun."

How stupid now for Jane to be hurt. And after all, if she is drawn to Simone, and would certainly love her own child, surely there is something to be said, and felt, for this small waif? Suddenly Jane herself feels abandoned.

"You don't need to decide, Lydia. At least not right now. I just wanted you to know I wouldn't be angry. I'd understand."

Although of course that wasn't her intention, and as it turns out, she might not understand so well.

"Guess what, I have something for your birthday. It's next Wednesday, right?" She meant this as a good-bye present, but now it's not. Or not for sure. Lydia will be ten years old next week. Not a bad time for making changes, shifts in decades.

By next Wednesday, Lydia's birthday, Jane's life will be utterly changed, one way or another.

From the bottom bureau drawer in her bedroom, where it's been folded right beside Brian's beige one, she retrieves the pink sweater she started planning weeks ago for Lydia, with the broad shoulders, the tucked-in waist, the fake pearl buttons.

"Thank you," Lydia says soberly, holding it up against her thin chest. Well, what did Jane expect? Embraces, or genuine gratitude?

"It suits your coloring wonderfully, I think," Jane says. "See how smart you look? Try it on." In the bedroom, she stands behind Lydia at the full-length mirror, her hands on the child's shoulders, smiling into Lydia's mirrored eyes, which aren't smiling back. "I made it myself."

"Yeah? Thanks."

They walk and ride the bus back to Lydia's almost in silence. Perhaps Jane has really done some damage here. It's so hard, setting out to do something, to know what will come of it. "Look," she says at the door, "I didn't mean you *have* to get another big sister, or that I want you to. I like being with you. I just wanted you to know you have a choice. Okay?"

"Really?" Lydia, looking up at her, seems so hopeful. Blundering Jane, not thinking, hurting a *child*, for heaven's sake. And really, mainly for her own convenience.

"Honest." She smiles down at Lydia. "See you next week?"

"Okay."

But how rash. Who knows what sort of state Jane will be in next week?

She passes the evening watching television. *Casablanca* is on. Everyone's favorite old movie, Jane's too. But look, here are all these law-breaking men, and some of them are heroes, right?

Still, it depends on the laws. It would be difficult to justify killing your wife. That's not exactly like resisting Nazis.

Real love can be a matter of principle, she can see that. It can be a matter of farewells in the face of a higher good.

What higher good can she see in giving up Brian, as if he were a box of particularly tempting chocolates? Only survival, maybe, and that's hardly selfless.

Sunday. Two days left.

Till what? A decision, at least.

Meanwhile, she writes down lists of jobs she has to do, and ticks them off as they're completed: pulling food, dishes, pots, from the kitchen shelves, wiping everything down, the shelves, the counter, washing the floor and the windows; then the living room, too, and the bedroom, out with the vacuum, polishing the glass-topped coffee table, dusting the wicker furniture and plumping its cushions, although of course that's just silly, since she'll certainly be sitting on them herself, shifting them out of place in the next couple of days.

The point is keeping busy. Because if she doesn't give her body enough hard, tiring jobs she has a feeling she's going to fly right out of it.

How do other people spend their Sundays? Maybe they watch football games on television. Some go to church. Probably there are some hearty types out, say, playing tennis in the chilly autumn sunshine, or raking leaves, or taking long deep-breathing walks for miles around the city, or canoeing on the frigid surface of the river. Things like that.

While here's Jane inside, all on her own, ferociously cleaning her apartment. The alternative is being outside on her own, with everyone else in pairs or groups.

When Brian comes, if Brian comes, they'll go out walking together. Then she won't mind being noticed.

She hopes he's presentable. But of course he will be, he's her Brian, the one she walks with. Once again she sees cameras on hand.

They'll take their own pictures, too, and spend evenings choosing photographs to be pressed into albums, sitting side by side on the loveseat, bent over the glass-topped coffee table. "Remember that?" they'll ask, smiling at each other, leaning, touching hands. Such memories they'll collect, the two of them!

Oh, she's slipped again, back into her pictures, forgetting for a few comforting moments that nothing may be what she has seen.

What should she still be doing with the apartment to make it exactly right? Just last-minute tidying, really. Buying more fresh flowers. They get more expensive these days, with winter coming on. She wonders if Mr. Alexander is back to work yet, recovered from his mugging. Will he be changed? She'll also have to buy food, and wine.

And, she supposes, beer. If it ends up going to waste, well, it will have been the least of her investments in all this. No need to decide, no need to panic.

Panic is caused by events coming to an inevitable close, and that isn't quite the case yet.

Not for Jane, but it's different for her mother. This seems like another loose end, like Lydia, or another chore to be taken care of, like washing down the kitchen shelves.

So she picks up the phone and dials, hoping she does better this time than she managed with Lydia, but just as unprepared. "Mother?"

"Jane! How nice to hear your voice. I was just thinking about you a while ago." Surprising enthusiasm, really.

"What were you thinking?"

"Oh, wondering how you were doing. What you were up to. I did tell you how much I like your apartment, didn't I?"

"Yes, you did. I do, too." How do other mothers and daughters talk? Are their conversations potent and personal, more to the point? "How are you?"

"All right. Nothing's too bothersome yet." By which she must mean she's not in a great deal of pain. "But I'm glad you called tonight. I'm starting the first treatments tomorrow, so I may be out of it for a while."

"How long?"

"Do they go on? Every day for a week. I'm checking into the hospital in the morning. I can start them here, and see how they go. If they don't work I might have to go to a hospital someplace bigger. Or not." How lighthearted she sounds. Or brave.

"Are you scared?" Jane is brave, too. She has never asked her mother a question like this before. She's trying to imagine how her mother's sitting, if she's all curled up on herself or relaxed on the sofa. Probably she isn't drinking any more, even for comfort, so there'll be no glass in her hand.

"Terrified. But to tell you the truth, the worst part's the waiting. It's awful not to be able to *do* something. At least tomorrow there'll be some action. So I'm scared, but I can't wait, too."

Well, Jane can see the sense of that.

"Would you like me to come and be with you? I could take some time off work." Rash, impulsive, and startling even to her. But think: it would mean she'd be elsewhere, wouldn't it? At least until the events she seems to have set in motion have taken care of themselves.

"That's very sweet of you, Jane." What's that in her mother's voice—surprise? Maybe gratitude? She makes Jane ashamed. "But I don't think so. I appreciate the offer, but there's nothing you could do and I'm not going to be fit company. I wouldn't want to be worrying that you were just sitting here with nothing to do. It's not the kind of thing anybody can really help with, I think. It's the kind of thing you have to go through alone."

Jane knows about that.

"If you're sure. But promise you'll call if you change your mind. I can be there any time." Until Tuesday night, that is. After that, it's too late. "So what happens this week?"

"Radiation. Then we'll see. Maybe surgery. I don't know which is worse. At least the radiation won't kill me, however awful it is. Anyway, after that, I can decide what to do from there."

Decide? "How can you make a decision about something like that?"

"I don't know, I haven't tried yet. But after all, I have to think about it. I'm not going to go on and on if it just means turning into a wreck. I couldn't stand that."

"Oh, Mum." Where did that come from? Or the sound of it, as if it came from a loving and sorrowful child.

This may be the last time they speak, think of that! Jane thinks of it, although she's sure her mother doesn't. Her mother has no idea she's not the only one facing something awfully real this week.

"I know, Jane," she says. "It's hard. I love you, too."

Jane can barely say good-bye for unspeakable affection. Hanging up, she bends over, weeping, for herself, and her mother, for having no words, for not knowing how to tell her what may happen, or how to comfort her for what is already happening. For everything, right at the moment.

But after all, her mother may live. So may Jane. Isn't it stupid to be grieving for something she never thought she had, like a mother or, for that matter, like a life?

14

On Monday, for the first time in her working life, Jane calls in sick when she really isn't. Brian has just one more day to spend in prison. She has just twenty-four more hours to decide. Perhaps she ought to go to work, if only to keep occupied, but some disconnection seems to have occurred over the weekend, separating her from what must have been real right up until Friday. Because this morning she can't imagine sitting at her desk or standing at the shelves or the counter doing ordinary tasks during these extraordinary hours. Nor can she imagine how she will ever again be able to sit at her desk or stand at the shelves or the counter doing ordinary tasks.

In fact, this morning she can barely put her mind to the library at all. Now and then she glances at her watch, or at the kitchen clock, and considers what she would normally be doing at this hour, and can even picture it, but so faintly, and from such a distance! There seems to be no history connecting her and the light and colors of the place, to the competent, quiet person who has been responsible for certain jobs. Right now, maybe she'd be typing a letter. And now perhaps chatting with Marcy; or

Mrs. Curtis might be giving her something to do. She can't quite call their faces to mind. Her absence may be causing something of a problem, since this is the day the library board agenda gets prepared: Jane's job. Still, she is unable to feel badly about calling in sick; it feels as if that whole life has belonged to some other Jane entirely, and her own whole life is here in this apartment now.

All those years ago, on Jane's first day at the library, when she was still young, she stood just inside the huge wood and glass front doors and breathed in—oh, she believed she was breathing in knowledge, and more than that, centuries of learning and wisdom. Leather bindings and crisp pages. She had a vague idea that all this would become part of the people there, that even without reading much of it herself, she would simply absorb it, given time. Effortless wisdom, or even salvation.

It was really only that the building was imposing and solemn. Unfamiliar. It didn't take long to realize there was no contagion involved, and that life inside the library was pretty much like life outside: all talk of husbands and babies and houses and roommates and dates. Perhaps that was just as well. Jane may have been left out, but could she have borne the burdens of either wisdom or salvation any better?

Still, her assumptions have probably been too extreme. Look at Marcy, for instance, with a life Jane never would have thought of. Also, not having read many of the books, Jane doesn't realize how many of them also speak of ordinary matters: husbands and babies and houses.

For once, she doesn't bother exercising. It's too late to improve any further the body that may or may not be important tomorrow. She drinks cup after cup of coffee, which doesn't improve her steadiness. Mainly she is sitting, waiting for something to simply present itself, so that she'll know.

She has been reduced to magic.

Her apartment is so still that she hears the sharp metal click of the mailbox downstairs. So this is when mail reaches here: in the morning. She's never been home to know that before. The possibility of a letter, however unlikely, rouses her briefly, so that she hurries downstairs, leaving the door open behind her.

And yes, here is an envelope, her address in that large, bold hand—why is he writing now, so soon before he's free?

Perhaps he's made some new decision of his own. Perhaps she no longer needs to be concerned. What if all this has been a waste?

Well, even so, it can't be, can it? Not now that she's learned a few things, not least of them what she can do with her hair and her face if she bothers.

"Dear Jane," it begins.

"Well I havnt heard from you so if I dont before Tuesday I guess I'll see you soon. Its real strange knowing I'll be out in just a little more time, like its a big blank after exept for seeing you, I dont know what wud be in my mind if I cudnt think about that. Its like these last days here arent real, I just go thru them trying not to let anything get up my nose no matter what happens (and somtimes thats real hard!!!) and just pitchur exakly what I'll do when I get out. Like go to the train and get a ticket and then I get on the train and maybe I have a cupla beers and then I'm in a whole difrent place and nobodys going to care because I'm free. Its been so long since I been free I cant remember it too well but I know its great!!! They got a guy here talks to guys getting out and he says be careful because its hard and I know hes rite but I dont care because I'm real sure this time.

"I'm kind of ashamed riting you that I still dont spell good enough maybe but you know what I mean I figure because I figure your real nice, there isnt a lot of people who wud help me like you said you wud. Exept like I said before dont worry if you change your mind, just let me know, I'll be OK anyways. If you all ready rote and said dont come thats OK but anyways I feel like riting, it makes me feel better.

"This week most guys here are treating me pretty much OK because getting outs a big deal everybody knows, so before they were bugging me but now there not because getting outs so close. I tell everybody here I really mean to go straight and they got to respec that, they know I'm going to be on that train to a whole difrent way and I wont be back here for sure!!

"Dont forget tho you can phone and I'll do somthing else instead of coming to your place. When I come I figure we got plenty to talk about, likely theres things you want to know about me, its nice you havnt ast so far.

"You know whats in my head tho is pitchurs of you and your place, it gives me somthing pretty to think about instead of here, so I can be strong. You know what I mean?

"So if I dont hear from you before Tuesday I'll see you then. I just wanted you to know I'm real excited!!! and thanks

"Sinserly

"Brian (Dexter)."

The sweetness of it! The need, the gratitude, the will and spine and backbone and hope Jane has already given to this man! All those exclamation marks! What enthusiasm!

What a responsibility.

It's clear from this letter that even though he still says it's all right for her to change her mind, he would be crushed. He would be left aimless, purposeless, hopeless, and the result, no doubt, would be criminal.

Still, when it comes to the point, she can't be expected to martyr herself to prevent injury to someone else. To Brian, or to anyone else he took it into his head to rob, say, or to beat.

But he means to go straight. He sounds so determined. She would save him, which has always been her intention. He's already grateful, so how much more grateful he could become as she pursued, they pursued together, his salvation.

This letter puts a terrible pressure on her chest. It weighs more than cement blocks, sand bags, anchors. And then on the other hand, it lightens her heart like a feather, like wings. How her life, so much changed already, could alter further! The changes so far have been, she would judge, almost entirely positive, except for occasional dread; so how could things go wrong if she just kept going to what seems, right at this moment, a natural conclusion?

Surely there could only be a continuing spiral of joy. Love, romance. All those good things.

He as good as promises to tell her all about himself when he gets here, and that's something, right? He intends to be not only straight but truthful. She can see why he wouldn't have wanted to tell her by letter. It's the sort of information that's best offered in person. Why, even that policeman didn't tell her by phone, he came right here to see her. Obviously it would be even more important to Brian to do so. So it really doesn't mean anything sinister, that he's never mentioned what he did.

He must wonder why she's never asked.

Anyway, the story as that cop told it is only one way of telling it: the facts. There must be a number of other ways, with more of the broad strokes filled in, so that standing back, a person could see an entire, more truthful picture.

Only of course that has to be done when the two of them are together. You can't paint true pictures with words, she understands that. And Brian's not that good with words anyway, on paper at least. (Not really a criticism, that; more an observation. No doubt he'll have other, compensating skills.)

He expects her place and herself to be pretty, he says. Perhaps, though, he means pretty of spirit, of heart.

She can barely imagine how he must feel. He may be as frightened, and as hopeful, as she. Just what are his pictures, anyway?

She could phone him tonight, if she wanted to stop him. Or early tomorrow.

Or she could phone to reassure him that he's welcome.

"Yes, of course you must come, the very moment you can, I can't wait," she could say. Or, "No, please respect my decision and deal with your own life. I can't take care of you although I meant to, but I don't think I'm the woman you have in mind after all."

There's still plenty of time.

The second, sea-blue-green sweater is well under way, the completed beige one wrapped in tissue and tucked in her bottom bureau drawer. It's good to have something to do with her hands, especially something connected with him. She's almost finished the second sleeve, and then she'll just have to decide whether the body should have a pattern, or be plain. The color, at least, is quite beautiful, but the body has to be so big! Plain might be better. On the other hand, a pattern would demonstrate not only her skills but her care. It's hard to know, but something will come to her, no doubt.

15

Plain, she decides. Quicker, for one thing, when there's so little time. For another, more concealing of bulk.

Still, pictures intrude as the needles flash. She's getting very fast at this, the sweater grows and grows, one row and then another and another, forming around the body that will fill it. Oh, the pictures! Brian, big and black-tempered, menacing, rough, cruel, sweet, gentle, and rehabilitated, so many conflicting qualities combining in odd ways, so that he may be rough and rehabilitated all at once, or black-tempered and sweet. Still faceless.

Now here's her mother, too, painted and in pain—what's happening to her at this moment? Has she had the first treatment? Is she right now weak and hurting, retching into a bowl at her bedside? Is any of that carefully styled hair already falling out?

And Lydia, wiry and beautiful and inscrutable, but more attached, perhaps, than Jane had dreamed, and more capable of sorrow. Little Simone, with her blonde hair tied back, Marcy behind her, holding her shoulders. All of them mean something to Jane. What a crowd, after all! Does she need any more?

There are all kinds of ways she could have chosen (could still choose) not to be alone, and not to be lonely. She does not, for instance, seem to have accomplished much good in the world, and it may not mean much that she likely hasn't done any great harm so far, either. If, finally, she felt the need to act, why did she undertake such a perilous, outlandish adventure?

She could become political, an advocate for the poor and disenfranchised; volunteer to serve in some overseas charity, feeding the starving, abstemious herself. She could go door to door gathering food for the hungry. She could abandon herself, in short, to the strenuousness of virtue. It's not too late. These are critical hours, but she still has time. And she's only twenty-eight. These extraordinarily dull years may have been leading to something large or even great, who knows? It's possible that with some effort, her goodness could equal her plainness.

People often assume the plain must be good. Is that a punishment or a compensation?

She also sees the tiny dark-haired creature who is the one, besides Brian, she has made up. This is not Jane's day for making distinctions between the real and the created.

If she does nothing, if she just keeps sitting here, knitting and drinking coffee, standing only to make more or to go to the bathroom—well, that's a decision also, isn't it? Doing nothing will propel events as surely as making a move.

She can pick up the phone or not: that's the deal. Brian will not come or he will. Action or inaction, but equally decisive.

This either is, or is not, a good time to create event, rather than lament eventlessness.

The day is slipping away. It used to feel as if her life were slipping away, but now it's all immediate, and hours have become as vital as years used to be.

Is this anything like how her mother feels? That dying (or believing she is dying) both slows time and speeds it, but at any rate gives each moment huge interest and importance?

Her mother didn't waste any time hopping on the bus and coming here to lay out what remains of her life like cards in front of Jane. Even so, she must also have spent some hours beforehand and even afterward grieving, rocking herself, trying to comfort herself. Death and love, it seems, may both require a degree of solitude. In the midst of either one, distraction could be dangerous.

Remember those warm hands of Jane's former companion, the faithful, sturdy silent one who lasted her for, really, a number of years? Perhaps she should have remained faithful to him, been satisfied with that harmless, compatible companion. Instead he has been replaced by Brian's shoulders, and his bones in the darkness.

But that companion, imperfect after all, could never have turned the trick of reality the way Brian may. Brian's shoulders truly are out there in these hours, on this day, as are his bones. In a very short time, his shoulders and bones may be right here beside her, in her living room, and then there may be further, and more critical, shifts and disappearances. Just as the Brian with whom she has spent the past months caused those warm hands to vanish, that Brian may be driven out by the one who knocks on her door.

Jane herself might be caused to vanish by the Brian who knocks on her door.

But really, what's the worst that can happen? Well, that's obvious. But if it turns out he is a dangerous and violent man, if it turns out that he tries to do to Jane what he apparently did to his young wife, all she would be abandoning, really, would be twenty-eight years of being plain and alone.

(Even Jane shakes her head sharply at this, irritated by such a level of self-pity.)

Of course the last moments would be nasty: painful and bloody, terribly emotional and revealing. Even without much to lose, she would no doubt fight back.

His wife probably fought back, and after all, she was just abandoning what, seventeen or so years, and maybe they were truly sad years she should have been only too glad to let go of. Still, Jane can see, against her will and better judgment, that ending: the young woman beaten bloody, hitting back more and more feebly, reduced to huddling in a corner, her arms drawn up around her head, curling around herself in the end, herself the only person who would try to protect her.

Maybe it's the kind of thing a person starts and then it gets out of hand and can't be stopped. He might have started with a slap and liked the feel of it, and tried a punch and liked the feel of that, and tried a kick and found that satisfying, and then kept on and on in search of new, improved sensations. He might have been quite astonished at the end to see what he'd accomplished. He might have been heartbroken.

Would he have been one of those men who did what he did and then called the police, sobbing and confessing?

He's had ten years to think about it. Does a scene like that get brighter or dimmer over a decade, do its outlines sharpen or blur with age?

Surely if he did nothing else in ten years, he would steel himself against a repetition. He would have to make promises to himself; something like, "I will never let something like that happen again, I will never get so out of control."

Perhaps this has only occurred in recent months. And when he felt himself to be a thoroughly safe person, he would have taken that step toward the outside world, placing his advertisement and reaching Jane.

That makes good sense. She is relieved to find a line of thought that makes good sense.

She has read that second wives can be lucky, benefiting from the training given their husbands by unhappy but adamant first wives. And if that's the case in ordinary circumstances, how much greater the benefits in this instance, when the first marital round was so extreme?

By and large, Jane might be safer with Brian than with almost any other man. Most men can't have tapped the depths of their violence as thoroughly as he has. Most women likely haven't, either. Jane has no idea what she herself contains by way of violence, but if she has certain kinds of passion, might she not have others also?

There could be considerable pleasure with a man who has investigated pain so thoroughly, couldn't there? What sensations a man like that might be able and delighted to provide!

For a moment, Jane believes she could cast away her life in return for such pleasures. Except that now this is no mere romantic possibility. This could be quite real, a different matter entirely, making her shiver.

Shivering makes her restless, and she sets down the knitting and stands. She starts to walk. Walking, she picks up things and puts them down somewhere else. She needs to *do* something. So she strips the bed and bundles sheets and underwear, towels and blouses, and heads to the basement and the washing machine. Upstairs again, she pulls the vacuum cleaner from the closet and runs it again over rugs and floors. Puts it away and sets out once more to dust: furniture, books, the television set. Back in the basement, she loads up the dryer. There is no sound from the downstairs apartment as she passes its door heading down and up; Jim must be at work. She still has no idea what he does for a living. Judging from his furniture, it's something well paid. Or perhaps that was all Steve, his income and tastes.

It would be very hard to live in a place furnished by someone else's income and tastes.

How will Brian like it?

Will? She stops tucking a clean sheet around the mattress, looks down at the bed, which may soon be her most vital piece of furniture. Has she decided, then?

No, it was only a slip. She's getting ready, that's all.

In her closet, she still has unworn clothes; those jeans, for instance, for those tender days when she felt a gentle Brian reaching out to touch. Wearing old slacks and a faded blouse, she sets out to wash the kitchen floor again.

She knows terrible things about him. But if he's been wicked, she is plain. A fair exchange?

She can still call, plenty of hours yet. Even tomorrow morning won't be too late.

If she phones, what? She would make the call; go to work; spend the day doing her usual jobs; buy a TV magazine on the way home; climb the stairs and unlock the door to this apartment; breathe in the silence and unbroken cleanliness, all this work she's done. At some point in the evening she would think, "Right now he might have been at the door. If I hadn't made that call."

By then she would have no idea where he might be, or how to reach him if she changed her mind again. It would all be too late. She would go to bed and see, feel, arms and shoulders and bones. She would know they could have been real. All this might break her heart.

On the other hand she would be safe, and she'd be in her own home, and she'd be surrounded by all the things she's chosen to surround herself with. If her heart were broken, well, she could likely learn to live with that.

Whatever decision she makes, the losses could be huge. With Brian, there is also the possibility that the gains could be huge. At least there's a chance.

None of this seems to be getting easier, does it? And already it's evening. The day has vanished and she's down to her last twenty-four hours. This is so hard! She would like to sleep and sleep, all the way to a decision, beyond a decision, so that by the time she wakes up, whatever is going to happen would have already happened.

But sleep, being desperately desired, is precisely what is beyond her. She pours herself one glass of wine, and then another. This feels pleasant, takes the edge off.

She has neglected to eat, but can't be bothered.

She picks up the book she's been more or less reading, but it's hard to keep her mind on words. And how unreal, the strong and sorrowful hero, the beautiful, patient, comforting woman. They'll be all right in the end. It's guaranteed that nothing terminally distressing can keep them apart. They don't even have to make their own decisions. Some writer, a formula, does it for them. That would be nice.

No it wouldn't. Well, but it might be.

Inevitability. It was a comforting concept.

Jane pours more wine. The bottle's running low. To-morrow she will have to get more. And beer as well, and hearty foods, like steaks. It's not as if anything needs to go to waste if she decides against him. With enough food in the place, she could shut herself away in here for days and weeks, never needing to go out. She could withstand any siege.

What siege?

Next thing she knows she's waking up to aching mus-cles, her body tilted sideways, her head leaning back onto a cushion, her neck and right side stiff and painful, a recollection of pounding, a lingering vision of fists. A small pool of wine has spilled and spread just below her breasts. Through the unshaded living room window she sees a red sunrise. This is the first time Jane has ever wakened like this: a new experience.

How will she waken tomorrow? In what situation, exactly?

She sits up abruptly. How could she have fallen asleep? She has wasted hours, when she should have been deciding. Now there's no time; if she is going to call and stop him, it will have to be almost immediately. Otherwise he'll be out and on his way, unreachable until he reaches her door.

But she doesn't have to answer his knock, does she? There are last minutes, like this morning, and true last minutes, like tonight. How far can she stretch this?

If he came, and knocked, and she didn't answer, he wouldn't break in, would he? Wouldn't he just turn qui-etly and sadly away? He would be disappointed, of course, after traveling all day with his hopes up. He might even be bitter and angry and hurt. He might go out and do something stupid and get himself arrested, and he'd be terribly disillusioned, but Jane herself would surely be safe. She could stay inside with all her supplies and be untouchable.

After that, she might never go outside again. There are places that deliver food, after all, and liquor as well, should she grow accustomed to that. She could simply stay here, on and on—not for fear of Brian, but just because, really, why should she go out? What good reason would there be even to move?

She can imagine that.

But she has a job, and a living to earn. How long could she go on ordering groceries, with no money to pay for them? How long could she stay here, with no money for rent?

Anyway, somebody, somewhere, would eventually notice her absence.

It's hard to imagine returning to the library.

She doesn't bother to call in sick today. She can't suppose they'd expect her, now that she's so changed. Although, she realizes vaguely, they have no way of knowing.

She doesn't look changed. Glancing into the bathroom mirror, she sees her face looking back, still plain, still ordinary.

She stands in the shower with her eyes shut, letting the hot water beat on her head, run over her plain features and her perfect body. It occurs to her that this is another place where she could spend the rest of her life, in this hot shower.

(Her spaces are getting smaller, aren't they? From little excursions into the world and work, to her apartment, to her shower. Where next?)

Hot water, though, runs out. She finds it both discouraging and encouraging, that nothing lasts forever. It's a thought that puts a little distance, some perspective, on decisions and events.

She dresses carefully, in one of the dresses that makes her feel like a movie heroine, a delicate drop-waisted mauve, with tiny flowers of pink and blue threaded through. In this dress she is in a romantic epic involving loss, falling leaves, wistfulness but, of course, still hope: knowing that the hero, temporarily mislaid, will reappear gloriously, making this small mourning worthwhile.

But she is running out of time for pictures, or roles in movies and books.

She brushes her damp hair dry, then curls it. She is getting the hang of this, the hairdresser was right, it's not so hard to maintain this style. Much more difficult is the makeup. She has been experimenting, but tonight she'd better get it right, the mascara, the foundation, the blush.

Is this a decision, then? Has she made up her mind?

Because it's too late to call now. She's spent far too long in the shower, and dressing, and brushing her hair, and now too much time has gone by, the morning is well advanced and Brian—well, what will have happened with Brian so far?

Probably he won't have slept very well, too keen for the hours to pass, too excited by freedom. At the morning's first sounds he would have been on his feet, waiting impatiently for routines—breakfast? exercise?—to be done. There must be a standard procedure for release: forms to be filled out, likely an interview with some official, words intended to warn or to motivate. He would change into ordinary clothes, no doubt out of style, out of date. Whatever possessions he arrived with—a watch, rings, wallet?—would be returned. Would there be a long corridor to walk down, accompanied by a guard, to freedom? In a movie there would be sunshine at the end. He would have to wait for keys to be turned, doors and gates to be opened. He would be carrying a small duffle bag, shifting it from hand to hand. And then would be outside. Breathing unbarred air. Standing on free concrete.

Thinking of Jane. Heading for the train station.

What pictures and expectations and plans are filling Brian Dexter's head right now, with regard to Jane?

So it is too late to call and stop him. Still though, she hasn't decided.

"Thank you for riting," he wrote in the beginning, "I enjoyed recieving your letter, it was kind of you to take the time." Later, "You must be a very kind person," and "I hope youll rite back to me soon because its real nice getting your letters!"

His spelling seems to shift somewhat according to his passion and excitement (and gratitude) of the moment. What else about him may be variable?

"It kind of feels funny you thinking I cud say somthing to help, I dont know what, also its hard just riting. Maybe it wud be easier if we cud be talking."

Maybe it would be.

"Like you say its hard to talk in letters its funny to know sombody and not know them too (exept I know you must be a very nice person but I all ready told you that before.)" She *is* nice; only untested.

"I guess we havnt rote a whole lot of letters but its like I know you pretty well do you feel that way too even if I havnt told you a whole lot? Anyways I see us sitting around and getting to know each other better and you sound like a nice person so likely it wud be easier for me to be nicer too."

Sounds reasonable. Sounds appealing. Sounds entirely possible, doesn't it?

"I'm kind of ashamed riting you that I still dont spell good enough maybe but you know what I mean I figure because I figure your real nice, there isnt a lot of people who wud help me like you said you wud."

Gratitude, hope—that's a good deal to work with, isn't it? More than some couples.

"When I come I figure we got plenty to talk about, likely theres things you want to know about me, its nice you havnt ast so far." And, "I just wanted you to know I'm real excited!!! and thanks."

On the other hand, she knows almost nothing about him. Just a few terrible facts, and some feelings from letters. Other couples, they've had time, and lots of opportunities to watch and gauge.

She keeps his letters in her bottom bureau drawer, in a pile alongside the sweaters, the finished beige one, the sea-blue-green one with only the back and the stitching-together still to be done.

Leaving the apartment, she hears her phone ringing as she locks the door behind her. Likely it's someone from the library, wondering if she's coming in. What will they think when there's no answer? That she's on her way to work? Gone to the doctor? Not sick in the first place? Dead?

After some days, someone might come around to check. Marcy, perhaps, on her way home from work. But not quite this soon. If Jane did die, how long before someone found out?

It's hard, shopping with no car. Meat and milk are heavy, and so are bottles of wine and beer. How bright and even painful the lights in the stores feel, and voices are loud and intrusive. She sinks gratefully into the bus seat, heading home. Her steps are slow, walking the last couple of blocks. Her arms and shoulders hurt, and her hands are shaking when she finally puts down the bags in her kitchen. There are angry red marks on her wrists, where the bags have been looped.

The day has moved on, and conclusions of some sort are inevitable; not only that, are coming on swiftly. And yet here is Jane, putting away cheese, milk, eggs, carrots, potatoes, and meat, one thing at a time, making space in the fridge to chill the beer, and laying wine bottles on their side, reaching to put cans in cupboards, folding bags and putting them away, neatly absorbing herself in detail.

There is simply nothing left to do. She has cleaned the place and stocked it. Her clothes and sheets and towels are laundered, the bed made up, the small lace tablecloth she bought weeks ago has finally found its place on the coffee table, and fresh blue candles stand straight in the crystal holders on the cloth. The place smells of cleaning fluids and sprays and polishes and flowers. Jane herself smells, she imagines, musty.

This time the shower's hot water isn't so comforting, and she is in and out quickly. Her hair, now washed twice today, is dry, flying out from her head, electric and brittle. Jane's hand, starting fresh with the makeup, leaps and trembles, so that she has to wash it off and try again.

Does the eyeshadow look foolish, the mascara over-done, the cheeks caked or clown-like? Does she look like someone trying too hard?

So more time passes in this way: washing her face and starting again. He may not even get here tonight, his letter said it might not be until morning. Could she bear another night not knowing?

By morning, though, her hair might be shining again. On the other hand, morning light is merciless. She would stand before him revealed.

If she opened her door.

She can't eat, can't read, can't focus on the television. Her disobedient fingers refuse to knit. She feels sick: truly as if she might throw up. This is exactly the sort of thing she could confide to Brian in a letter.

But oh, there'll be no more letters! What a very sharp pain that is! It hasn't occurred to her before that there will never again be a day when she comes through the door downstairs and looks at the mailbox and sees the glint of white envelope through the slits. There won't be any more evenings spent writing down her life, to send hundreds of miles to a perfectly understanding companion. Now there's a loss to grieve for.

Well, lots of people get attached and addicted to rituals of one kind and another: pouring drinks, lighting cigarettes, the day's first cup of coffee. Jane might have been better off smoking.

What time do trains arrive? She could phone and find out, but is afraid of sharpening her apprehension further.

Several times she stands and goes to her bedroom to look in the mirror. Even with makeup she seems pale. She might pinken in different clothes: a pale pink blouse with long, loose sleeves, and a slightly deeper pink skirt that reaches almost to her ankles.

She does look healthier, and she is taking steps. Having made these preparations, can she ignore the knock on the door, if it comes, if she chooses?

If it comes? Could Brian change his mind? Again, she hasn't taken him into account, has given him no life of his own at all.

What heartbreak, if he didn't come. How devastating if a choice never presented itself; if, even without seeing her or knowing a great deal about her, Brian, perhaps whimsically, simply wandered off elsewhere.

It's now quite dark outside.

With the television off, it also seems unusually quiet; although perhaps she doesn't usually listen this keenly. Only a couple of birds are still making sounds, and a very faint line of music trails up through her floor from Jim's apartment. Does he remember what night this is? Is he listening, too? Is he thinking about her at all?

Cars pass the house now and then, but not often. Occasionally there are footsteps on the sidewalk, and she tenses.

These are the last sounds of the first twenty-eight years of Jane's life, and she wants to listen closely. She pulls a straight chair to a place just inside the door, near the raised front window. She sits with her legs crossed at the ankles, her knees carefully together, her hands holding each other tightly in her lap. She hears her own heart beating, and believes she can even follow the sounds of her blood moving swiftly through her body. This is an-other moment that could go on infinitely, she feels. She could sit here forever.

Imagine all the other sounds out there! Rockets and guns being fired in countries an ocean away, the cries of babies being nibbled at by rats or hunger, the roars of men, enraged and violent, and the keening of women mourning their dead. Playful sounds, too: little girls skip-ping rope and laughing, little boys rolling on dusty play-grounds.

Lydia whimpers in her sleep. Lucy sits hunched on her sofa, her feet on the coffee table as she paints her toenails with a tiny swishing brush sound.

Jane's mother takes a glass of water from a nurse and washes down a pain-killer. Her hand absently brushes her body, looking to the source of her disease, or trying to heal it.

Marcy kisses Simone good night. Simone giggles, high-voiced and full-throated.

Jim, playing old favorite songs of his and Steve's, is making himself so sad a tear falls onto the back of his hand with a little plop. No, he isn't thinking of her.

Brian listens to rhythmic train wheels and conversations. Or to his own footsteps in the train station, with voices on loud-speakers calling out destinations. Or he is outside the station, looking around at the city he's landed in, taking it in.

In bedrooms everywhere there are cries of ecstasy; although in other rooms, there are also cross, impatient voices. Jane, listening so carefully, hears a great mixed choir of invitation and life. She is amazed it seemed silent before.

She knows she will easily hear through this din, however, particular quiet footsteps. She will hear them first on the sidewalk, then downstairs in the hall. Men's boots, but not heavy or menacing, moving slowly and firmly to her door.

Even so, because she is sitting right here at the door the light knock is startling. She was right, she does just drift into events; even this has turned into more of a drifting than a decision. So much time spent wondering, when as it turns out, she simply stands and opens the door without thinking.

Inevitability.

He's bigger, stockier, than she'd expected. Older-looking, too, even a bit grizzled; or perhaps just unshaven. His eyes are quite a sharp blue, even in the dim light of the landing. He is wearing jeans, somewhat baggy, and a plain white T-shirt and a brown leather jacket. His hands, though, are oddly slim and shapely, long-fingered. Ragged fingernails.

He is clean. She can smell something sweet on his skin. He must have stepped off the train and washed his face and hands, and splashed on aftershave.

Might he not have shaved, while he was at it? But there is, after all, something male about bristles, the stubble of beard. He does look unnervingly male.

Oh, but while she scrutinizes him, what is he seeing? Is he taking in at a glance the sum of her plainness, or is it a matter of details and particular features? Is she anything like his pictures and impressions? She can't tell from his expression, can't read his face.

Faced with him, she can no longer recall her own pictures and impressions.

Is he appealing?

What has she done?

Here he is at any rate, arrived finally at her sanctuary. His hand is on the door. Jane feels dizzy with terror, excitement, horror, and hope. No more pictures.

"Come in," she says, inevitably (we all knew, didn't we?), and steps aside.

❦

Well good for Jane, then. Good for Brian. May he linger here in benign and rehabilitative love; may plain, deserving Jane finally be cherished, by whatever means the two of them devise. Look, she's pouring herself a glass of wine, and handing Brian a beer. Now they're sitting down beside each other on the wicker loveseat. You can't expect them to be at ease, and if Brian doesn't seem to know quite what to do with his legs or his arms, well, he's a big man in a fairly small place. And if Jane is curled sideways, her legs tucked up, leaving a space between them, well, she often sits like that. They are looking down at the drinks in their hands, not at each other. It's a hard scene to interpret.

Still, here they are, starting off on something. Probably they should both be proud of having taken steps, at least, toward new lives. He wrote his advertisement, she noticed and answered. He pledges reform, she promises love, as she understands it.

He possesses true shoulders and hands; she dips her head, so that he won't see her face too clearly. She turns the wine glass with her fingers, he tips back his head to drink beer from the bottle.

He smiles, but it's hard to make out just what sort of smile it is, besides being somewhat strained, and that's only natural. At any rate it's a start, and Jane smiles back, sweetly, she hopes.

He has deep lines bracketing his mouth, and tiny ones at the edges of his eyes. Does this mean he likes to laugh, or do the lines come from some source she has, as yet, no way of deciphering? Of course he's uncomfortable; he has come here with a purpose, and whatever that is, he must need to appear harmless and benevolent. It's a strain, trying to give a good impression. Jane is finding it a strain, too, trying to convey warmth and welcome without words. How much can be read from expression and feature and posture? Dismayingly little, after all. Having imagined that just to see him would make the future clear, she is surprised to find that this is going to be more difficult and complicated than she thought.

He has, sitting, an unexpected roll of flesh that stretches the T-shirt over the top of his jeans. His hands . . . she shivers, staring at those long and narrow fingers, at where they've been, where they might be. They have a horrifying history and a hopeful future, and here they are, holding a bottle of beer she has bought, as he sits beside her on her wicker loveseat, his bulky legs crossed, one toe tapping at her glass-topped coffee table.

What is he doing here?

Jane's heart is very busy. Like a conjuror she has made this man appear, and it seems he may still be her creation. All those little steps she's taken, and none of them felt terribly real compared with this. Here he is, real as anything!

Does he feel anything like this? He must have conjured her, as well, and now here he is with his creation, in the flesh. Is he puzzled or astonished that she turns out to be real?

She does hope he isn't disappointed. She isn't disappointed, exactly, only stupidly startled.

All this may turn out as right and true as Jane has ever dreamed. Her pictures may be perfectly correct—look what she's brought to life so far, right here in this room.

If so, she will have to be cautious with her visions, because who knows what may turn out to be magic?

It's hard to think of something to say. He's silent, so it must be up to her. It surprises her to be able to speak, to be able to take this responsibility. But it has been her intention to relieve him of his burdens, and this is just the first of them. She can still imagine he will absorb her burdens, also. It's heartening, surely, that he is here and she still has all these hopes.

"I made you a sweater," she tells him, "and started another." He looks pleased, and possibly grateful. She's glad she has something to offer. "I didn't know if you'd have many clothes. They're plain, but I hope you like them. I hope they fit. Let me show you."

She sets down her glass, uncurls her body, and stands to go to the bedroom where her gifts to him are waiting. And so they begin, launching themselves, as even the least brave and most fearful must do every day, into their entirely mysterious futures.